Pleading His Belly on Zakon-4

E.J. LeRoy

The Whumpy Printing Press

Cover Design by Nicole Alessi

To my readers

Contents

A Note About Content

Our main character, Henry, is a devout Catholic and his faith plays a major role in this story.

Additionally, this story contains the following content:

Imprisonment

Forced nudity

Alien sexual content

Dubious consent

Male pregnancy

Religious guilt

If this book isn't for you, no worries! But if it is, we hope you enjoy this story about a hapless spice merchant ...

Chapter 1

"Henry Trevalu, you are under arrest for transporting illicit drugs to Zakon-4 with intent to distribute."

I blinked, staring at the Zakonian customs officer. He may have technically been humanoid, but it didn't ease my nerves any that his scaly red, yellow, and black skin resembled a venomous coral snake. His sharp teeth weren't reassuring either. "I'm sorry ... what?"

The customs officer read from his tablet. "Henry Trevalu, upon entering port you have declared yourself to be the sole proprietor of the cargo ship *Neon Durango* and fifty percent owner of Trevalu Intergalactic Spice Company. Do you deny this?"

My breaths grew short. It was too late to deny anything considering the Zakon-4 Port and Customs Department already had my identification on file along with my previous verbal affirmation and customs documents. I swallowed, forcing myself to stay levelheaded enough to make sense of this absurd declaration of arrest. Thus far, no one had put handcuffs on me or looked about ready to. Keeping my mouth shut might prevent that from happening. Ignoring my silence, the customs officer spoke in a calm, unsettling tone as he continued to read from his tablet.

"According to your own ship's manifest, you are carrying vast quantities of illegal narcotics. For this reason, you are under arrest."

You would think that telling a guy he was under arrest for the second time would trigger klaxons, station-wide panic, and umpteen guards charging the checkpoint with guns drawn. In fact, the Zakon-4 PCD boasted no more chaos than usual. Merchants and vacationers from all over the galaxy shoved their way through long lines, emitting a cacophony of languages and generating heat. The stuffiness of the overcrowded building really made me regret wearing sweats. According to *Professor Prendergast's Intergalactic Travel Guide, Fifth Edition*, this was supposed to be Zakon-4's cold season. But the combination of thousands of people squeezed into an undersized space and my rapidly increasing heart rate created a sweltering atmosphere.

"I'm not transporting any narcotics," I said, trying to keep my voice level. "You said you read my ship's manifest, right? *Neon Durango* is a cargo ship for *spices*, not drugs. You know, lotiki, momiti, hathgaar, coriander, cinnamon, those kinds of things."

"And poppy seeds?"

I wiped the perspiration off of my forehead with the back of my hand. "Yes, of course, poppy seeds. They're a popular spice all over the galaxy. Well, they're a fruit, actually, but I don't want to argue about semantics." *Certainly not when I'm being accused of transporting narcotics to a planet with a "zero tolerance drug policy."* "Look, officer, maybe somebody framed me by hiding drugs in my cargo. It's a big port. Things like that can happen, right?"

"You have not been falsely accused. As of yesterday, poppy seeds are classified as a hard drug on Zakon-4."

"That's ... that's impossible." My heart lodged itself in my throat, threatening to choke me. Didn't *Professor Prendergast's Intergalactic Travel Guide* state that Zakon-4's anti-drug laws were some of the harshest in the galaxy? If the custom officer's statement was true, I was looking at a literal death sentence!

"It is not impossible." The customs officer's voice conveyed no emotion. "It is the law as of yesterday."

"But there's no way I could have known that en route." I forced myself to take a deep breath before passing out. An abundance of perspiration running down my back made my sweats cling to my skin. If I didn't find a way to talk myself out of this, I would be playing a starring role in one of those alien prison dramas I watched during the flight – for real. "What if I just return to my ship and dispose of the poppy seeds before attempting reentry to Zakon-4?"

"Ignorance of our laws is not a valid defense. And you have already entered our port with the poppy seeds among your cargo."

Thoughts failed me, leaving me to sputter. "But ... but ..."

The customs officer subtly moved his hand under his desk, like he was pushing an alert button. My chest and stomach clenched. Instinctively, I looked for an escape route. Maybe if I disappeared in the crowd, I could sneak back to *Neon Durango* and get off this vile planet.

Please, God, I prayed, *give me an exit. I don't want to be killed for a technicality.*

A large, magenta-skinned alien woman with enormous cheeks resembling a Bubble Eye goldfish elbowed her way to the front of the line, practically knocking me over. She held a potted female kiengar plant in full bloom, its distinctive rank odor making me nauseous and dizzy.

"I have been in line for more than two standard hours waiting to enter Zakon-4," she said to the customs officer, puffing out her cheeks to their maximum size.

I didn't wait to hear the continuation of her complaint. Her revolting plant aside, that irate, pushy woman was a speedy answer to my prayer for escape. *Thank you, Jesus*, I prayed as I slipped into the crowd. Fewer than ten seconds later, sirens blared. An alert issued over the PA system in three languages: Universal I, Zakonian, and English. While snaking through lines and avoiding anything wearing a uniform, I tried to focus more on making a clean break from the Zakon-4 PCD than the endlessly repeating announcement. The clear, booming voice of the woman behind the microphone made it impossible to block out the message completely. As I ran down the stairway leading to the hangars to locate *Neon Durango*, the alert cycled around to English again:

"Attention all persons in the Zakon-4 Port and Customs Department. There is a fugitive in our building wanted for drug transportation and trafficking. Description of the criminal follows."

The criminal? I panted, far more afraid than tired. For the Zakonian authorities to declare me as a *criminal* rather than a *suspect* further emphasized the severity of Zakon-4's legal system. As far as they were concerned, I was already guilty before the trial began. Would I even receive a trial if caught? I pushed myself onward, shoving past a crowd of reptilian children on some sort of intergalactic field trip.

"Name: Henry Francis Trevalu. Species: Human. Sex: Male. Age: Twenty-two standard years. Height: 1.65 meters. Weight: 57.61 kilograms. Skin color: White. Hair color: Dark brown. Hair length: Long. Eyes: Blue. Facial hair: None at this time. Scars: None. Tattoos: None. Piercings: None."

Thanks to my meticulous record-keeping before reporting to customs, Zakon-4 authorities had an exact description of my identity and appearance. Not to mention I must have been captured on camera at some point. I pulled my hair back and stuffed it into my hood. It wasn't *that* long, but anything I could do to alter my appearance would help.

"If you see this individual, report to authorities immediately," the announcement continued as I made my way down a second flight of stairs. "Do not attempt to detain him yourself."

Great. Way to make me look like some deranged career criminal who's too dangerous to arrest without help from professionals. Speaking of professionals ...

I tapped out an emergency alert on my watch. Hopefully, the Earth Embassy on Zakon-4 could get me out of this mess. A digital acknowledgment popped up, hovering above the watch for maximum readability: *Your emergency alert has been received by the Earth Embassy of Zakon-4.* After that, the message disappeared and nothing else happened. *Why am I not surprised?*

"Check the ships," someone said nearby, making my heart jump. "He might attempt to steal one or return to his own."

I ducked into an unlocked room that turned out to be a cramped, stuffy broom closet. The nondescript, vaguely humanoid, metallic cleaning robot behind me flashed a light blue light in five second intervals – sleep mode. Sharing a room with a form of artificial intelligence wasn't a great idea, but there weren't any alternatives at the moment. My second attempt to contact the Earth Embassy resulted in radio silence, not even an acknowledgement this time. *Think, Henry. Think!*

Too desperate to be embarrassed, I placed a collect call to my dad's office and lowered the volume. *Come on, come on. Pick up the phone. Please, Lord, don't let Dad be at a meeting.*

"Trevalu Intergalactic Spice Company."

Dad's voice gave my heart wings. *Thank God, he answered.*

"Dad, I'm under arrest at the Zakon-4 PCD," I whispered. Okay, so technically I was at large, but there wasn't time for clarification.

"Under arrest? What for?" I could easily imagine Dad jumping out of his chair at that moment, ready to send a fleet to collect me with him leading the charge.

"Zakon-4 classified poppy seeds as hard drugs the day before my arrival. I've read their laws. They're going to kill me, like really *kill* me." Stating Zakon-4's death sentence for drug traffickers out loud made my whole body freeze. For an instant, it was as though all time stopped. I didn't even breathe or have a heartbeat. Execution wasn't a theoretical danger anymore. Not even when I fled from customs did my brain fully comprehend the stark reality of my situation: *They are going to kill me.*

A flash of blue against the door turned my flesh to ice. My throat tightened as though my own body was trying to strangle me. When I realized the burst of color was merely a reflection from the sleeping robot's intermittent sleep mode light, I willed myself not to sigh aloud with relief. Footsteps from patrols in the hangar pounded against my eardrums. They weren't in front of the broom closet, but judging by the direction and volume of the patrols' muffled chatter, they would be soon.

"Henry, are you there?"

I swallowed back a hard knot. My voice threatened to crack like a teenager's. "Yeah, Dad. I need a lawyer, fast."

"I've already sent an alert to Mr. Finley. Hang in there."

Mr. Finley was one of several lawyers Trevalu Intergalactic Spice Company kept on retainer. Oddly enough, I didn't know his first name because I met him when I was a kid, back when I had to call everybody Mr. So-and-So or Ms. So-and-So. For whatever reason, that didn't change with Mr. Finley, and I never heard anybody call him anything else all these years. Knowing him, he probably *insisted* on being addressed with an honorific by everybody. I just hoped that pompous intergalactic trial lawyer earned his pay when it counted the most.

"Thanks." I forced myself to take deep but quiet breaths. The humidity of the broom closet and my shallow breathing left me lightheaded. Sweat soaked through my clothes. "I tried calling the Earth Embassy on Zakon-4, but – "

The glowing light reflecting against the door turned from blue to red. *Uh oh ...*

"Intruder!" the robot said, its eye and mouth slits glowing red. "Intruder in the hangar!"

Crap.

Chapter 2

Of course, it was only a matter of time before the PA system's fugitive announcement linked with the on-site robots. The cleaning robot shot out its arms like some creature in a midnight monster flick. I wrestled with the doorknob. It refused to budge. The robotic alert must've triggered the electronic lock. That didn't stop me from trying to rip it off like a madman. The robot stepped closer, probably intending to squash me between itself and the door.

"Henry, what's going on?"

While trying to escape from the broom closet, I forgot that Dad was still on the line. Rattling the doorknob in vain, I called out, "I'm trapped!" To the robot I said, "Stop! Don't crush me!"

"Henry, stay on the line!" As though Dad suddenly turning into an emergency dispatcher could change anything.

"You're not allowed to hurt a sentient being," I said to the cleaning robot, hoping that my statement was correct. On a planet cruel enough to execute someone for transporting poppy seeds, it wouldn't surprise me if robots were allowed to do Zakonians' dirty work. Would this metallic janitor reach out and crush my throat? Not knowing how else to protect myself in a tight place with no escape routes, I dropped to the floor and curled up in a ball. Prayer was my last line of defense, so I used it.

"Hail Mary, full of grace, the Lord is with thee ... "

The robot bent down and yanked my crossed arms away from my chest. I cried out and then resumed my prayer as it hauled me to my feet. Fear dampened my perception of pain. My heart beat so hard, I wouldn't have been able to stand unless being forcibly held upright. Somehow, I managed to keep praying Hail Marys aloud. Dad overheard me and joined in, probably trying to bolster me as well as care for my soul in case this proved to be the end of my too-short life.

Without warning, the robot pulled my hands behind my back as though handcuffing me. Pain seared through my shoulder blades from the quick jerk. Something popped but thankfully didn't break. My watch phone call disconnected automatically on account of the swift movements imposed upon my slight frame. The robot's grip on my wrists made me grit my teeth. If it squeezed much harder, I'd wind up with bone fractures.

"Henry Francis Trevalu is in custody." The robot must have been linked into an automatic communication system with the authorities because it didn't need to touch any equipment to issue the announcement. "Please collect the criminal from the broom closet in Hangar 3."

"Let me go." Even if I wanted to take a commanding tone, the rattling in my ribcage prevented me from speaking louder than a strained whisper. "Robots aren't allowed to harm sentient beings. If you turn me over to the authorities, I will be executed. Do you understand?"

The robot merely repeated its announcement that I had been captured and to please collect me from the Hangar 3 broom closet. While waiting for a sentient creature to arrive, I prayed some more, wishing I had taken time to memorize the official Act of Contrition.

The doorknob stirred.

I'm sorry for all my sins and hope to live in Heaven with You for all eternity. Amen.

Two Zakonian police officers entered the broom closet, scarcely leaving me room to breathe. The robot released my wrists, only for the guards to bind them behind my back with glowing, tracking handcuffs. I didn't have time to read the model number, but those cuffs probably had the ability to deliver electric shocks if I attempted another escape.

As the police led me out of the broom closet, letting the robot return to sleep mode, I expected them to spout off a list of charges against me. They said nothing. On the way up the stairs, I stole a glance at *Neon Durango*. While hiding in the broom closet, I had been so close to my vessel. Now, it was surrounded by Zakon-4 authorities. Perhaps it was stupidly sentimental, but *Neon Durango* was my first private cargo ship, a sixteenth birthday present from Mom and Dad. I named it after my two favorite rock bands: Neon Spark Plug and Durango Hacksaw. At least Neon Spark Plug still produced awesome music; Durango Hacksaw had become a joke. Odd thoughts to be having while walking up the stairs to one's doom, but they came to mind nonetheless.

Getting marched through the Zakon-4 PCD should have been a humiliating experience, but my mind raced with questions about Mr. Finley. Would he be able to win my trial for me? I mean, Dad wouldn't have chosen him if he thought Mr. Finley would let his son get executed on a hostile alien planet, right? And what about Mom? Did Dad tell her right away about what was happening, or did he take some time to think about how to best convey the news? Was it a case of, "Honey, please sit down. Something urgent has come up. It's about Henry." Or was it more like, "Where's that good-for-nothing Mr. Finley when I need him? Dang it, Henry got arrested for transporting poppy seeds and is going to get murdered for it!"

I swallowed, trying to make my heart calm down. All this adrenaline had to dissipate sometime. Hopefully it would stick around long enough to keep me on my feet. My legs trembled slightly. *Oh no.* That was the first sign of an adrenaline rush ending, wasn't it – weakness and bouncing in the legs? *Please, God. Don't let me collapse before we get to wherever the police are taking me.*

"Look, Mama," a gray alien child said, tugging on her mother's arm with one hand and pointing to me with the other. "That's a human. I saw one in a picture book at school."

The mother shushed her child and pulled her away from the customs line while the police dragged me through the crowds.

Trying to keep my focus off of my faltering legs, I noted the demographics at the Zakon-4 PCD. There were maybe five other humans in the distance, but most of the building's current population consisted of Zakonians plus a smattering of other races from throughout the galaxy. Other than that child who recognized my species from a picture book, few paid me much attention. When we finally made it outside, a large red car idled at the curb. From my previous reading of *Professor Prendergast's Intergalactic Travel Guide*, I recognized it as a Zakonian police car.

My escorts shoved me into the back of the vehicle, not taking care to prevent injury. I hissed when my head bumped against the door seal. One of the police officers grabbed my cuffs and locked them into a restraining device behind me, putting pressure on my wrists and lower back. This was no way to transport a prisoner. An accident or even a sharp turn could lead to dislocation or spinal damage. On top of that, my legs started bouncing from the aftershocks of adrenaline.

While the police drove, I stared at the empty seat beside me. For some reason, it reminded me of how my mom used to tell me when I was little to leave some space for my guardian angel. "Of course, they don't *have* to sit, being angels, after all," Mom used to say, "but it's a nice way to show your guardian angel that you care." The memory forced a smile out of me despite the sharp ache induced by my restraints.

I haven't really given you much thought lately, have I? I prayed to my guardian angel. *Well, if you'll forgive me for saying so, the Angel of God prayer sounded like sissy stuff by the time I was eight or nine years old. But no hard feelings, right?*

Of course, there wasn't a verbal reply to my impromptu, apologetic prayer, but my legs didn't shake as much as before. My heart still raced but not quite as badly.

I winced as we hit a bump in the road. The motion jerked on my wrists.

Uh, Guardian Angel? I know I've been giving you the silent treatment for a few years, but would you please protect me on the way to wherever we're going? I'd rather not arrive with broken wrists. And, um, if I get to our destination in one piece, I'll say the Angel of God prayer tonight, okay?

We didn't hit any more bumps in the road. After a while, the police parked in front of a large, gray, imposing building with Zakonian writing engraved on the façade. This had to be either the courthouse or the Zakonian equivalent of a county jail. One of the policemen unhooked my handcuffs from the car. He and his partner each took charge of one of my arms to make me ascend the steps leading into the foreboding edifice. I swear the entryway looked like a giant alien tongue ready to pull me into its mouth and swallow me alive. But my wrists, although sore, weren't fractured as far as I knew. It looked like I owed my guardian angel an extra special prayer tonight.

Chapter 3

The inside of the building was as intimidating as its exterior – maybe more so. Depressingly gray walls, dark floors, metal furniture, and wide open spaces sucked any possibility of joy out of the room. Even more disheartening were the long benches lined up against the walls, occupied by approximately ten chained prisoners apiece. A few benches held Zakonians but most seated a diverse collection of alien species, some of which I couldn't identify. I doubted it was a coincidence that the benches with Zakonian prisoners didn't include any aliens. *Professor Prendergast's Intergalactic Travel Guide* said Zakonians had a reputation for being a xenophobic lot, and this display of segregation seemed to confirm it. Moreover, aliens vastly outnumbered Zakonians, suggesting highly disproportionate rates of arrest.

The police walked me past the benches to a desk at the back of the room that was manned by another Zakonian.

"This is Henry Trevalu," one of the police officers said. "He is under arrest for transporting illicit narcotics to Zakon-4 with intent to distribute, specifically poppy seeds. Because this is a capital offense, we have decided not to press additional charges against him for evading the authorities."

The Zakonian sitting behind the desk yawned. "Yes, yes. I already know about Henry Trevalu. His lawyer called, some human by the name of Mr. Finley."

My lips twitched into an involuntary smile. If Mr. Finley got to work on my case this quickly, then surely I would be exonerated.

"I also received a message from the Earth Embassy," the Zakonian behind the desk continued, scrolling through his tablet.

So, the Earth Embassy on Zakon-4 did *respond to my message.* My skin tingled with hope.

"Of course, their word carries no weight around here, so their threats of igniting a media scandal are of no account."

And ... there goes that little spark of optimism.

"Never mind that," one of the policemen said. "When is Henry Trevalu's trial date?"

"Given that the lawyer needs time to travel, it will have to be one standard week from today. I've already scheduled it."

"One standard week?" I said. "That barely gives Mr. Finley enough time to arrive on Zakon-4 and pass through customs, let alone defend me properly in court."

"We pride ourselves on speedy trials," the Zakonian behind the desk said, his voice sharp. "Our system of justice is efficient."

And full of swift executions, no doubt. But I wasn't in a position to argue, so I said nothing.

"Officers, take the prisoner to be processed. I already have him checked into the system." The Zakonian stationed behind the desk made a dismissive gesture and then returned to whatever he was doing on his tablet – probably playing video games for all he cared about justice.

My two police escorts led me down a long corridor full of locked doors. It looked more like a creepy motel's hallway than a courthouse. One of the police touched his watch against a door to unlock it. Upon entering, I was surprised that the room was much larger than expected. Its interior looked like a somber clinic complete with an exam table and medical devices.

One of the police officers removed my cuffs and the other confiscated my watch. Blood rushed to my hands, drawing a groan. When I rubbed my wrists, the skin near the base of my thumbs hurt the worst. No question, bruises would pop up tomorrow.

"All right," one of the Zakonians said. "Enough of that. Take your clothes off."

I froze. "Um ... what?"

The other Zakonian seized my forearm and jerked me toward the exam table. "You heard him. Take your clothes off."

My breath hitched. It wasn't as though I'd never been in a locker room or anything, but this was different. Wasn't it horrific enough getting arrested for transporting poppy seeds and threatened with the death penalty on an alien world? Now I had to get naked to be scrutinized by two alien cops? And with all those medical devices in the room, Heaven knew *what* they intended to do with me.

"Don't you have something for me to change into?" I said, my heart pounding. A new layer of sweat soaked my clothes. It should have been a relief to remove my drenched sweats, but not under these circumstances. "Like, don't I get to wear a hospital gown or something?"

"You'll get your prison uniform when we're done. Now, are you going to undress by yourself, or are we going to have to do it for you?"

The thought of two alien police officers ripping my clothes off gave me enough incentive to comply. If there was no way to avoid this indignity, I wanted to exercise at least *some* control over my own body.

It'll be okay, I told myself as I removed my sweatshirt. One of the policemen immediately took it. The coldness of the room permeated my skin, making me shudder. My captors' impatient stares induced another chill.

"Take your pants off. Hurry up."

The harshness of his voice startled me into instant obedience. He whisked away my sweatpants while one of the legs still pooled around my ankle, tripping me. Instinctively, my hands shot out to grab the exam table. Otherwise, nothing would have broken my fall – except maybe the unforgiving floor. As it was, regaining my balance put me in the awkward position of arching my back and sticking my butt out for a moment to keep from toppling over. Righting myself may have only taken a second or two, but my face burned with the realization that I had unintentionally displayed myself like a prison punk.

Prison punk? The thought almost made me hyperventilate. It hadn't occurred to me until that moment, but a lot of those benched alien prisoners looked pretty big and rough. What if one of them tried to rape me? *Oh, St. Agatha, spare me that!*

"Underpants too, come on."

I turned away from the Zakonian police as I grasped the waistband of my briefs. If my stomach and chest weren't tingling with ants and butterflies, getting ready to expose my backside would have made a great form of defiance – a promise of a white full moon on an otherwise moonless night. *Hah!* But my silent gallows humor did little to reassure me. Who was I kidding? Turning away wasn't resistance; it was self-preservation from full-frontal nudity.

Almost all prisoners in the galaxy have to go through a similar process for intake and searches, I told myself to muster some courage while removing my underwear. *And, well ... if my Lord and Savior had to face His tormentors naked, then I have nothing to be ashamed of either.*

Not that I intended any blasphemy by the extreme comparison between my situation and His crucifixion, but the image helped me disassociate from what I needed to do. Giving a little thought to my often neglected guardian angel made it easier to bear the humiliation when one of the police officers grasped my shoulders, spun me around, and practically threw me onto the exam table.

"Lie flat on your back, arms at your sides." When I didn't position myself to his liking, the Zakonian hissed, spewing saliva close to my face. "Quit covering yourself with your hands. Do we need to restrain your arms in order to run the full body med-scan?"

"No! Don't tie me up. I ... I'll be good."

I clenched my fists, shivering from cold and fear. Never in my life had I been so exposed and vulnerable. An ominous hum emanated from the exam table as well as overhead. Right, this room was equipped with a double bio med-scanner to capture all my stats. Focusing on the ceiling's med-scan beam as it traveled along my body from head to toe didn't take the edge off of my discomfort as I hoped it would. The slight heat of the other scanner's beam running from the back of my head toward my legs chilled rather than warmed me. If anything, the sensation of being scanned from both directions as though lying inside a giant copy machine worsened the feeling of being abused. I closed my eyes, praying that my invasive prisoner intake exam would end soon and that something could restore my wounded dignity.

The dual med-scan beams powered down. Their residual heat dissipated.

"No weapons, diseases, illicit substances, or contraband detected," one of the policemen said after reading the results on his watch.

I shifted into a fetal position and pulled my knees close to my chest, trying to create some privacy. A short time later, the other Zakonian handed me a thin, light blue prison uniform consisting of a shirt and pants but no underwear or shoes. The back of the uniform was stamped with thick black letters in Zakonian and Universal I. While I couldn't read the Zakonian, the Universal I bore a stark statement: PRISONER AND PROPERTY OF ZAKON-4 STATE JAIL.

I dressed quickly, despite the shaking in my hands and legs. Although no one had touched me inappropriately – with the possible exception of shoving me onto the exam table – my tear ducts started to swell. Besides the forced nudity and full body scanning, what sentient being wanted to be labeled as "property"? I swallowed hard, forcing the emotion down into the pit of my stomach. Crying wouldn't help. In this environment, tears could be perceived as weakness and endanger me. *Dear Guardian Angel, please keep me safe under your wings ...*

"The prisoner has been processed and cleared for transportation," one of the police officers said into his watch. "Send two guards to Room 17 for pickup."

While waiting for the two guards, I sat on the edge of the exam table and stared at my bare feet. Were they really going to leave me without any socks or shoes? Come to think of it, those benched prisoners didn't have anything to cover their feet either. Not that I expected any floor hazards wherever those guards were going to take me, but if the coldness of the inmate exam room provided any indication, the temperature wouldn't be ideal.

As expected, two Zakonian guards arrived.

"Your prisoner." One of the officers tugged my sleeve to make me get off of the exam table. Fearing how rough he might get if his patience were tested, I stood without delay. Because I had been sweating so much, the floor didn't feel too cold under my feet. "House him in the alien male section, wherever you can find space."

Wherever you can find space? It sounds like they have overcrowding problems ... The back of my neck prickled. If prison dramas and documentaries were to be believed, overcrowding meant high tension, frequent violence, poor hygiene, and rampant disease.

Each guard grabbed an elbow, pulled me out of the exam room, and led me down the hall. As we passed through the depressing corridor, one of the doors was ajar. Hulking sobs overlaid with arguing Zakonian voices carried in my direction. I caught a glimpse of the blobby alien on the exam table as well as the gist of the Zakonians' source of consternation: they were having trouble verifying the prisoner's sex even after performing a battery of tests.

That poor alien, I thought as the guards steered me down another hallway leading into a basement. *It was bad enough going through one full-body scan stark naked, but multiple tests?* My eyes welled up in empathy, but I gulped down the barely formed tears. I regained control of myself as we descended the stairs. Before the jail cell came into view, cries of anguish and the stench of species-diverse male body odor drifted toward me.

This was going to be my home until my trial next week, where if I lost, I would be executed. *God help me.*

Chapter 4

Maybe "jail cell" was too nice a term for the room where the guards dumped me. "Somewhat modern dungeon" would have been more appropriate. By my count, there were twenty-five of us non-Zakonians (i.e. "aliens") stuffed into a noisy, smelly, bare gray room with no bedding and a single toilet with a built-in water fountain/sink. There was an overhead light, but no windows because the cell was in the courthouse basement. The primitive ventilation system combined with the overflowing number of prisoners made the room hot and stuffy. Apparently, I shouldn't have worried about being barefoot.

Of the twenty-five prisoners, only two appeared to be of the same species – a couple of reptilian humanoids with raspy voices and forked tongues. The others exhibited a dramatic range of sizes, shapes, and features, most of whom outsized me. An alien resembling a giant polar bear but with a gorilla's hands grunted and seethed close to the cell door. If that guy had a temper, I was toast. He looked like he could crush my neck with just two or three fingers. Some of the other prisoners looked almost as intimidating. Claws, sharp teeth, tentacles, acidic slime ... I held back a shudder as the ugly, primal fear of rape resurfaced. *St. Agatha, may your divine intercession protect me ...*

An Elbaren flopped around near the middle of the cell, barking like a sea lion. His struggle distracted me from my terror. Some of the prisoners made way for him as he galumphed toward the toilet. I tried to make space for him too without stepping on any other prisoner's toes – or equivalents of toes. Although Elbarens were a subclass of mammals capable of breathing underwater or at the surface, they didn't do well on land, at least ~~not~~ in terms of mobility. After all, they were just about the closest real-life examples of merfolk in the galaxy, albeit with webbed fingers.

Wedged between other prisoners trying to make space, I couldn't help facing the Elbaren as he hauled himself onto the toilet. Most of the prisoners averted their gazes, but the cramped quarters made it impossible for some of us to offer the alien a modicum of privacy. I closed my eyes out of respect, but the sound of a heavy gush startled me into opening them. Even though I turned my head, I caught a glimpse of milky white fluid splashing over the side of the toilet bowl onto the floor.

Some of the prisoners made noises of disgust or yelled at the Elbaren for making a mess. The Elbaren barked back at them in his own language and slapped his sides in challenge. I scooted away from the thick of the conflict, protecting myself from a potential fight but also feeling sorry for my fellow inmate. Unless I was mistaken, this was spawning season for Elbarens. The males couldn't help releasing copious amounts of sperm this time of year, often multiple times per day. In the ocean, that wouldn't be a big deal. Here, in a high stress environment, biological functions could lead to murder.

Please, God, protect the Elbaren from harm. What happened wasn't his fault.

A scuffle ensued, pushing me toward the cell door, too close to that polar bear/gorilla alien for comfort. My heart stopped for an instant when the beast made eye contact. Then, to my extraordinary relief, he lumbered toward the Elbaren and nudged him away from the toilet. Oh, the big guy just needed to go. Maybe because of the alien's humungous proportions, the fight between the Elbaren and some irritated prisoners failed to escalate beyond posturing. The offended parties grumbled and returned to their previous locations. *Thank you, Jesus, that the fight never happened.*

Once the immediate danger passed, I forced myself to breathe deeply despite the revolting mélange of odors, trying to get my heart rate back on track. Even without the threat of violence, the atmosphere remained tense. Prisoners sized each other up, some talking trash but backing down before a real fight could break out. Most made a lot of noise, probably as a means of asserting dominance. You know, male chest-thumping behavior in its various forms – definitely not my thing. Few made an effort to create a bubble of calm and quiet, which was what I craved more than anything. Well, besides my freedom, of course.

Through the grunts, snarls, hisses, agitated conversations, shouts, swearing, and other unclassifiable noises reverberating throughout the cell, I distinctly heard a constant, low rumble like a distant siren. What in the galaxy was making that haunting sound? Come to think of it, wasn't that the first sound I heard when the guards brought me down to this basement holding cell – something like angst personified?

Wait a minute, I thought. *That sounds like a Lularian in howl.* If that was the case, the weakening cry meant its owner didn't have long to live if everyone continued to ignore that biological alarm call. This was basic Intergalactic First Aid 101. But apparently, no one was going to bother providing care. Either that, or the other prisoners didn't understand the gravity of howl. The guards obviously didn't care, or they would have done something about it ages ago. *Time to put my Intergalactic First Aid training to good use.*

I inched my way from the cell door to the back of the room, taking care not to ignite a brawl by accidentally elbowing, bumping, or stepping on someone. Praying a Hail Mary in my head as I crossed the room, I made it to the other side without incident. Sure enough, lying against the back wall was a Lularian staring blankly at the ceiling. An involuntary, mournful cry emanated from his chest. It lacked the force of early-stage howl, meaning he must have been in this pitiful condition for hours. Bruises marred his moon-white face and arms, suggesting that one or more irritated prisoners had smacked him around in an effort to silence him.

My heart ached for my fellow prisoner. Lularians were only the sweetest and gentlest humanoids in the universe. Their total nonviolence, honesty, and fair business dealings made them excellent customers and vendors, not to mention wonderful friends. Trevalu Intergalactic Spice Company engaged in a great deal of trade with their noble race. It was always an honor and a pleasure to work with them. But their inherent kindness also made them targets for predation by more aggressive alien species, as evidenced by this prisoner's injuries. Before contact with other worlds, Lularians didn't have words in any of their languages for most acts of violence, certainly not for "murder" or "rape." And they always responded to those in need, not just from goodness but their biological imperatives. After all, without regular affection, a Lularian could literally die.

How did a Lularian end up in a place like this? Then again, I'm on my way to the death house for transporting poppy seeds ...

Despite the cramped conditions, I managed to kneel beside him. *Okay.* I took a steadying breath and thought back to my training. *Start by squeezing his hand.*

Just like an unconscious human needing CPR, a Lularian in howl constituted implied consent for treatment, so I squeezed his hand in gentle intervals to mimic a resting heart rate. If he weren't in the late stages of howl, just holding his hand would have been enough to snap him out of it. On Lulara, anyone who heard the howl would instinctively rush to hold the hand of a fellow Lularian in distress, so the medical condition would never get this bad – unless the howling Lularian happened to be deep in the wilderness alone for some reason.

The howl continued, so I placed my other hand on the Lularian's forehead and spoke to him soothingly. "It's okay, man. I'm here. I'm Henry Trevalu. Maybe we met in passing during an intergalactic trade show, huh?" I ran my fingers through his matted, snow-white hair, continuing to squeeze his hand at the same time. "Come out of howl now. You're not alone."

An almost gagging sound replaced the howl.

"Easy, man. I've got you."

The Lularian groaned and closed his eyes. His chest quit rumbling. When his eyes opened, I smiled with relief. Who would've thought that my Intergalactic First Aid 101 training would actually save a sentient being's life?

"Greetings and blessings upon you," the Lularian said. "My name is Traiyo."

"Greetings and blessings upon you too, Traiyo. I'm Henry Trevalu, in case you didn't hear me earlier."

Traiyo smiled. "Thank you, Henry, for saving my life." He held fast to my hand. I continued stroking his hair to keep him from slipping back into howl. According to Intergalactic First Aid 101, maintaining contact for at least five standard minutes after recovery was crucial to prevent a relapse. "I tried not to fall into howl, but the stress of captivity overpowered my will."

"Hey, man, that's not your fault. Someone should have responded to your howl hours ago."

Traiyo gasped for air, racked with aftershocks. "I believe some of the inmates responded with blows, trying to shut me up."

A well-placed swear word to condemn such cruelty would have been appropriate. If it weren't for the inevitability of one of Traiyo's assailants overhearing me, I would have said it. Instead, I inhaled through my nose, sucking the rising anger into my lungs. Hurting a Lularian was almost as heinous as punching a baby.

Traiyo squeezed my hand, probably sensing the strength of my emotions. "Don't trouble yourself, Henry. Focus on surviving. Besides, I won't be here tomorrow. After my trial, I'm getting deported."

"Deported? You're sure that's going to happen?"

Traiyo rubbed his thumb over the top of my hand. Whether he was attempting to derive comfort or impart it, I couldn't say. "Few prisoners win their freedom here on Zakon-4. It is because I published and distributed a treatise saying so that I will be returned to my home world. The trial will be nothing more than a formality."

While providing aid and aftercare, my own trial had receded to the back of my mind. Once Traiyo stated the dismal outcomes of the Zakonian justice system, all my concerns turned inward.

"What do you mean few prisoners win their freedom?" I said, way too loudly for being in close quarters with twenty-four other guys. "I got arrested for transporting poppy seeds and might get the death penalty for it!"

Everyone in the cell went silent. All of the inmates stared at me. It was eerie, awkward, and frightening all at once. Considering that I was holding another guy's hand and stroking his hair made the situation worse. What if they saw my compassion as a sign of weakness, an invitation to attack? For several seconds, nothing happened. Everything and everybody became unnaturally still. Then, the polar bear/gorilla alien took a step toward me. The other prisoners got out of his way, and I didn't blame them.

"Henry Trevalu, was it?" Polar Bear/Gorilla said in a low, grumbling tone.

I nodded, unable to find my voice. It was tempting to release Traiyo's hand to straighten myself to my full height, diminutive as it was. But I couldn't release the Lularian despite my vulnerable position, knowing that doing so before five minutes passed could hurt him.

"No one here will harm you." Polar Bear/Gorilla jutted his chin out as he looked at the other inmates, issuing a warning. "A man destined for death is entitled to some small comforts."

"Thank you." My words came out as a pathetic squeak.

"You all hear this?" Polar Bear/Gorilla's voice rattled the small space as he addressed the prisoners. "If Henry Trevalu needs to relieve himself, you better get out of his way so he doesn't have to wait. If he needs a place to sleep, you better give him yours. At shower time, you better back your butts up to the wall to let him be first on the chain. And anyone who lays a finger, claw, or paw upon him will answer to my wrath. Is that clear?"

The prisoners all murmured in agreement. I said nothing. Polar Bear/Gorilla returned to his preferred position by the cell door. Other inmates resumed their varied chatter. While tending to Traiyo, ambivalence about my new status as a protected person seeped into my core. On the one hand, these favors could make the next week a whole lot easier. On the other hand, what would be the price of accepting them? Was Polar Bear/Gorilla enforcing deferential treatment out of respect for my bleak upcoming judicial sentence, or was he actually grooming me for assault? Nothing was free in jail, after all. That's what they always said in prison documentaries and TV shows. More than that, Polar Bear/Gorilla's speech laid bare my stark reality: I was going to die.

Chapter 5

The lack of a clock or natural light made it impossible to determine the passage of time. No doubt, this was by design, to further disorient us. At least Traiyo was able to tell me when he had recovered sufficiently for me to safely let go of his hand and stop petting him. Once he sat up on his own, I knew he would be all right. After that, I relieved myself, too full in the bladder to care that other inmates stood so close to the toilet by necessity. Thankfully, none of them watched, following Polar Bear/Gorilla's orders.

When I finished, the Elbaren whimpered behind me, grimacing and beating his tail against the ground. The poor guy needed to release sperm again. Spawning season had to be the worst for his kind. I got out of his way, which was far easier after Polar Bear/Gorilla's speech; everyone parted for me like Moses and the Red Sea.

"All right," someone said outside the cell a long time later. "Strip down and line up for shower time."

None of the inmates hesitated to remove their sweat-soaked clothes. I followed suit. After being treated worse than an animal for only a few hours – had it been a few hours? – any sense of modesty took a back seat to a desperate need for cleanliness. While the prisoners established positions in a bunched-up line, Polar Bear/Gorilla nudged me toward the front. A Zakonian guard carrying a bundle of restraints and armed with a possible shocking device entered the already overcrowded cell. Another guard stood outside at the ready in case of trouble. The guard who entered our cell clasped a stretchy device around my ankle and looped it through a chain. Then, he moved on to the next prisoner in line and did the same, linking him to me with the same chain.

So, this is what Polar Bear/Gorilla meant when he told the inmates that I would always be the first on the chain, I thought while waiting for the rest of the prisoners to get attached. Looking back, I noticed that the Elbaren got chained on the wrist since he didn't have legs. What a sad bunch we were, though – twenty-five naked prisoners from around the galaxy getting herded off to take a shower, looking like one of Earth's old chain gangs.

A quick march down the hall and we were in a huge room with one long shower. One of the guards attached the ends of our chain to the floor and turned on the water. Half of the showerheads turned on, soaking us. It became clear pretty quickly that this wasn't going to be a real, leisurely shower. This was a hose down. Following the automatic water rinse, the second set of showerheads rained soap on us. I scrubbed up as best I could, as did most of the other inmates. The two reptilian humanoids yowled and cursed. Most likely, soap didn't agree with their scales. Only the Elbaren emitted sounds of pleasure – no surprise given his aquatic origin.

Another quick spray of water to wash off the soap, and that was the end of shower time. Then, some overhead fans kicked into high gear, drying us off. After that, the guards led us back to our cell. A cleaning robot exited the cell while we were getting unchained. Clean prison uniforms lay folded near the back of our cell, surprising me. Another pleasant surprise was a thin futon-like mat covering the floor of the cell. Once the guard slammed the door behind us, inmates rushed to get dressed, buffeting me in the process. Polar Bear/Gorilla roared, making them freeze. They stopped and stared at me. Apparently, I was going to be the first to get back into uniform – another privilege for the almost-condemned.

The overhead light shut off. *Lights out, I guess.* Even getting first pick, there wasn't a good place to sleep in the cell. All of us had to lie on the floor, trying to squeeze into a cell stuffed far beyond its maximum capacity. I lay on my side, not just out of habit but to leave space for the others. The Elbaren scooted in behind me and Traiyo lay in front. It was fortunate Polar Bear/Gorilla lay on the other end of the cell because his furry body would have given off way too much heat to sleep. As it was, feeling the Elbaren's rubbery, merman-like body pressed up against mine disquieted me. Traiyo leaning into my front was only a little less awkward. The rest of the prisoners found areas to curl up side by side or on top of each other, equally cramped.

As I drifted off toward an exhausted sleep, I remembered my promise to my guardian angel. Silently, I prayed an Angel of God and then thanked the saints and Jesus for keeping me safe so far. *Please don't let me die*, was my last prayer while drifting out of consciousness. *I don't care what it takes. Just please don't let me die.*

I woke up with something cold and sticky on my back. Behind me, the Elbaren whined and then galumphed toward the toilet. The overhead light snapped on, increasing my awareness. *Ugh ... that guy just jizzed all over the back of my uniform, probably in his sleep.* Even worse, I realized that my morning hard-on was stabbing Traiyo in his lower back. Mortified, I rolled away from him and whispered my daily prayers: one Apostles' Creed, one Our Father, three Hail Marys, and a Glory Be. For good measure, I added an Angel of God.

"Wha ... ?" Traiyo said, rolling toward me. "Did you say something?"

"Oh, uh, nothing. I was just praying."

"Oh."

Traiyo sat up and then stretched. If he felt my ... condition this morning, he was enough of a gentleman not to mention it.

The rest of the cell's occupants awakened – yawning, stretching, and the like. A guard rattled the door to alert us to his presence and then let himself in. I knew better than to ask for a clean uniform. From everything I had experienced so far, Zakonians didn't grant favors.

"All right. Line up for exercise time."

Again, the inmates cleared the way to let me go first. What was intended as a courtesy just made me feel worse, like everybody felt sorry for me that I was likely going to be found guilty of drug trafficking within the next week and sentenced to death. Still, I took what few comforts I could in this dismal place. If my impending, near-certain execution meant getting to be first in line, using the toilet whenever I needed, and having first pick of sleeping spots, I would roll with it.

As soon as the guard finished chaining us together, he led us to a room resembling a gymnasium. Lest anyone think exercise time meant playing sports or running freely, I assure you it was more like old Earth notions of exercising prisoners – making us walk in a circle, pausing, turning, bending knees, stuff like that. It was just enough to keep our muscles from withering to nothing but not enough to make us strong. While we engaged in this pathetic, mandated workout session, the Elbaren's sperm dried, making the back of my uniform itch.

Back in our cell, the sleeping mat had been removed and replaced with a breakfast tray for each of us. Prisoners snarled and fought over the meager rations, although no one dared touch mine with Polar Bear/Gorilla keeping watch. Traiyo shoved about half of his food onto my tray.

"Eat," he said. "My trial is this afternoon, and I'll be sent home. But you'll need your strength. Besides, I owe you my life."

"Thank you, Traiyo." I wolfed down all the food, as awful as it tasted, and still felt hungry. My stomach growled.

While the rest of the inmates finished eating, a guard arrived to take Traiyo and two other prisoners to trial. Some of the remaining prisoners moved as though ready to fight over the removed prisoners' food scraps, but Polar Bear/Gorilla bellowed, making them halt. All looked at me again. Too hungry to exercise Christian charity, I claimed all the abandoned food as my own – my privilege as a nearly condemned man. Minutes later, when the ache of hunger gave way to satiation, guilt drove me to remorseful prayer. What right did I have to eat my fill when so many others went hungry?

God forgive me, God forgive me, God forgive me…

Chapter 6

The next few days passed exactly as the first: sleep, exercise, breakfast, boredom, lunch, more boredom, dinner, shower, lights out, sleep, repeat. Only the cast of prisoners changed. Every day, some guys got taken away and others got locked inside. From observation, eavesdropping, and engaging in conversations, I learned that the average time spent in jail before going to trial on Zakon-4 was only two to three standard days. My week-long stay was unheard of and that was only because the Zakonian court needed to wait for Mr. Finley's arrival. By the end of the week, none of the prisoners I encountered on my first day of incarceration remained. Still, knowing that I was destined for death row, all of the incoming inmates paid their respects, upholding the privileges Polar Bear/Gorilla established for me.

Finally, my court date arrived. It had only been a standard week as promised, but my muscles and bones ached as though I had waited a hundred years. Sharing that ridiculously thin communal futon with an average of two dozen guys per night wasn't exactly conducive to sound sleep. Since daily shower time didn't include shaving, my face hosted a week's worth of stubble. As the guards marched me directly into court, uniformed and barefoot, I swayed from near constant hunger and weakening muscles from the lack of proper exercise. It was in this sorry condition that Mr. Finley saw me for the first time since I was a free man.

"Henry?" Mr. Finley said, wide-eyed, as I sat beside him in court. The guards just sort of plopped me beside him and then retreated to the periphery of the courtroom. "Oh, man, you look terrible."

"Really? What did you expect?" I said, rubbing my eyes after a sleepless night filled with worry about my upcoming verdict. "Where are Mom and Dad? Didn't they come with you?" Surely my parents would arrive soon to offer moral support. As of that moment, the courtroom was mostly empty.

"Your parents are waiting outside the courthouse." Mr. Finley took his tablet out of his briefcase, way too matter-of-fact for my liking given the circumstances. "Zakonian court doesn't allow spectators."

A Zakonian man wearing a long red and black robe entered the room – the judge, I presumed. He was followed by a dozen Zakonian men and women dressed in similar robes. They took their seats on either side of him. The judge remained standing.

"Henry Trevalu, you stand charged with transporting illicit drugs to Zakon-4 with intent to distribute, the sentence for which is death. How do you plead?"

Mr. Finley cleared his throat and stood on my behalf. For the umpteenth time since my arrest, I prayed that he spent his time wisely while traveling to Zakon-4 over the course of a week, learning everything he could about my case and Zakonian law in order to get me exonerated.

"Zakonian Grand Councilman and Council, I am entering a plea of not guilty for my client, Henry Trevalu, on the grounds that he did not and could not have received ample warning to dispose of the poppy seeds in question before arriving at the Zakon-4 Port and Customs Department. Poppy seeds were declared illegal one day before his arrival and – "

"Your client's ignorance is not a proper defense." The judge – or Grand Councilman, rather – tapped something on a tablet. "According to records presented by the Zakon-4 Port and Customs Department, the classification of poppy seeds as a narcotic or 'hard drug,' as you *humans* might call it" – (the way he spat out the word "humans" gave me a serious chill) – "occurred more than eighteen standard hours before Henry Trevalu's arrival. That was more than sufficient time for him to have read the new law before arriving."

Mr. Finley pulled up something on his own tablet. "It is also on record that no incoming cargo ships received an alert regarding this legal change."

The Zakonian Grand Councilman huffed through his nose, clearly losing his patience with my lawyer. "You are an intergalactic lawyer, are you not?"

Mr. Finley's Adam's apple bobbed. "Yes, Grand Councilman."

"Then you of all people should be aware of the basic fact that Zakonian law does not require informing cargo ships of any legal changes. It is the responsibility of the captain or merchant in question to research any applicable laws before docking. Your client had eighteen standard hours to do so and failed to do it."

That ... wasn't good, to say the least. Sweat beaded up in places I didn't think had sweat glands. My heart rate went from resting rate to a marathon run in a second. Using my trembling fingers to keep count, I mentally started reciting a Rosary of the Sorrowful Mysteries, praying for the intention that Mr. Finley could find something, *anything* to get me out of this predicament.

Mr. Finley's lower lip twitched. The tick was subtle, but I knew that he had exhausted his arguments for the defense – me. Worse, that bungler stated openly in court that I transported an illicit substance to Zakon-4. My ignorance of the criminalization of poppy seeds was the best he had to work with? What the heck was he doing during his week-long flight to Zakon-4, filing his taxes?

"Have you anything else to say before the Grand Council and I deliberate?" the Zakonian Grand Councilman said after an excruciating pause.

"Yes, Grand Councilman," Mr. Finley said. "I demand my client's right to an appeal."

"On what grounds?"

"On the grounds that there be sufficient time to prepare for proper legal proceedings."

"You have already had sufficient time to prepare for *this* trial. In fact, we scheduled the trial date to give you adequate time to arrive in order to defend your client."

You said it, I thought, hardly believing I was taking the Grand Councilman's side with that statement. *How could Mr. Finley have done such a terrible job when he enjoyed a whole week in space to devote himself entirely to studying the intricacies of Zakonian law? Some intergalactic trial lawyer he turned out to be!*

"Grand Councilman, think of the intergalactic scandal this case has caused. The Earth Embassy on Zakon-4 has been pleading for my client's release with the assurance that they will transport him off-planet permanently. You would never need to see him again."

"Surely a man of your legal background knows that the Earth Embassy has no jurisdiction over our courts, nor do the media or public opinion."

"But Grand Councilman, I must insist that – "

"Enough! My colleagues and I will now deliberate." He left the room with the rest of the Grand Council in tow.

It was so tempting to rant and rave at Mr. Finley, to tell him what an incompetent, blundering fool he was. Instead, I devoted that energy to fervent prayer. Nothing short of a miracle was going to get me out of this, so why waste breath on the worst lawyer in the universe?

The Grand Councilman and his lackeys couldn't have been gone more than ten or fifteen minutes because I was just moving on to the Glorious Mysteries when they returned.

"Stand up, both of you," the Grand Councilman said. Mr. Finley stood, looking pale. I grabbed on to the desk in front of me to keep my balance as I stood. My legs threatened to give out from under me.

"Henry Trevalu, for the crime of transporting illicit drugs to Zakon-4 with intent to distribute, this council finds you guilty and shall apply the maximum penalty of death."

I wasn't hearing this. The way my head swam from the verdict, this had to be a fever dream. Nobody really got sentenced to death for drugs anymore – let alone poppy seeds! This was all theater, and something or someone was going to save me at the last possible moment. There was going to be a huge *Deus ex machina* moment where someone would burst through the courtroom doors to say, "Wait! There's been a terrible mistake! The time zone and date lines were misrecorded. Henry Trevalu actually arrived the day *before* poppy seeds were made illegal on Zakon-4. Therefore, this is a case of *non-rétroactivité de la loi pénale*. Grand Councilman, Mr. Trevalu cannot be charged with a crime before it became a crime, and therefore his case must be discarded and the man must be freed!"

But this wasn't the movies. No one rushed to the rescue.

"Given the unusual circumstances, you will receive an appeal one standard month from today," the Grand Councilman said. "In the meantime, you will be held in custody at Kalka'ahn

Maximum Security State Prison. Guards, escort the prisoner outside for transport."

The Zakonian guards closed in on me. If I wanted to make an escape, this would be the time, while I wasn't being restrained. But I couldn't make myself run. With my legs shaking like a newborn lamb's and no place to go, I had no choice but to submit myself to being handcuffed.

While being hauled outside over the grainy sidewalk, still barefoot, to the prison transportation van, I caught a glimpse of my parents standing behind the courthouse gate. They clung to the fence, eyes on me. If they called out, I didn't hear them. I was deaf to everything but my own heartbeat and desperate prayers for mercy.

Chapter 7

Intake at Kalka'ahn Maximum Security State Prison was similar to Zakon-4 State Jail. I was ordered to strip naked, get scanned, and change into a new uniform. This time, I didn't hesitate to shed my clothes for total strangers. Shame didn't register in my brain anymore. All that ran through my mind was a nonstop replay of my horrific sham trial.

Henry Trevalu, for the crime of transporting illicit drugs to Zakon-4 with intent to distribute, this council finds you guilty and shall apply the maximum penalty of death.

The Grand Councilman's words would remain stuck in my head like a bad Durango Hacksaw song for the rest of my prematurely shortened life. Was this because I claimed other prisoners' food scraps instead of stepping aside for needier inmates? Was helping Traiyo not enough to build merit in order to preserve my corporeal life? Not that I aided him for any reward, but surely that was worth something in the eyes of the Lord? Knowing that my saving Traiyo's life might be counted as a heavenly treasure didn't comfort me. I mean, yeah, getting to Heaven technically mattered more than life itself, but why did I have to get killed for something as stupid as poppy seeds? That wasn't even receiving the grace of being a martyr of the faith!

Immediately after processing, the guards took me to a small room with a screen. They permitted me one video call with my lawyer.

"Henry, I'm afraid I have some bad news," was how Mr. Finley started the conversation.

Bad news? What could be worse news than receiving a death sentence? Unless ... Oh, Heaven help me! "What? Have they cancelled my appeal? Please tell me they haven't cancelled my appeal."

"No, the appeal is still scheduled."

I let out a breath I didn't realize I had been holding. "Don't scare me like that!"

"But I'm sorry to say that your appeal appears to be a formality. I've been doing some research, and it seems as though the only reason for granting an appeal in the first place is to give the Grand Council time to ... Well, I'm going to be frank. They're using this time to determine the best method for executing a human."

I threw up in my mouth a little and ended the call early. The guards escorted me to a cell that had only one other prisoner in it, a tentacled alien. Before I could get a good look at him, the guards tossed me in the cell and turned on the force field. For some reason, the zapping noise of the security device made me start ranting like a madman.

"Can you believe I'm going to be executed for transporting spices that were made illegal only one day before my arrival on Zakon-4?" I said to my alien cellmate, who lay in the bottom bunk on the other end of our cell. He resembled a somewhat humanoid, bipedal octopus with big black eyes like those little green Roswell aliens in old Earth fiction. His red skin and pink suckers pulsated. If I weren't so preoccupied with my impending death, my cellmate's biology would've creeped me out a bit. But after a week of being stuffed into a Zakonian jail with approximately two dozen alien men per day only to get sentenced to death afterward, I was beyond caring about appearances. And after a week of not being able to shave or exercise properly, I didn't look so hot either.

"Seriously, this backwater of a planet outlawed poppy seeds, classifying them as 'hard drugs.' Is that crazy, or what?" I don't know why I bothered venting to my alien cellmate who may not have been listening, understood, or cared. A harsh laugh escaped my throat. "Outlawing poppy seeds ... Good joke, huh?" Yep, I was officially losing it.

"Some good my family's lawyer did," I continued, pacing to strengthen my legs. At least this cell had space to move and bunks to sleep in. Although I'd rather spend a whole year in my last jail cell if it meant avoiding execution. "You'd think that being the heir to Trevalu Intergalactic Spice Company would've afforded me better legal counsel, but no. Apparently, when Zakon-4's trade and tourism division's literature said, 'zero tolerance drug policy,' they weren't kidding. Even the threat of an intergalactic diplomatic crisis didn't convince them to offer leniency."

Already tired from walking so much after having next to zero meaningful exercise in the last week, I eased myself onto the floor and ran my hands through my tangled hair. Funny how I didn't notice before how matted it was. Here I had been worried about a week's worth of beard growth when the hair on my head made me look like a deranged castaway. My breath probably reeked too – no toothbrushes or mouthwash at Zakon-4 State Jail either.

"My appeal is next month, but my lawyer says not to get my hopes up," I said, unable to stop my mouth from running like a faucet. "It's just a formality. Really, the delay is for the Zakonian Grand Council to figure out the best way to execute a human." Visions of being lethally injected, gunned down by firing squad, or shoved out of an airlock made my heart pound in my ears and a shockwave zip down my spine. My mouth popped open, wanting to scream but unable to find the right noises. All that came out was a pathetic squeak and a useless plea for mercy. "I mean, come on, man. I'm only twenty-two Earth years old. That's way too young to die!"

My cellmate merely twisted his tentacle arms in reply. The pink suckers on their undersides pulsated. Then, he rolled over in his bunk, appearing to go to sleep.

With nothing else to do and no one else to talk to, I prayed a whole fifteen-decade Rosary on my fingers, pleading with Jesus and His Blessed Mother to save my life. Of course, I wanted to go to Heaven someday, but did it have to be a month from today by violent means for a bonkers reason?

After I finished my prayers, a guard returned with a food tray and a dark blue towel that had something rolled up in it. He shoved both items in my arms and left, leaving me to balance them. Too hungry to be curious about the towel's contents, I shoved the bundle aside and ate. Just like in jail, the food was lousy. I wasn't sure why my cellmate wasn't served a meal, but maybe he had already eaten. And honestly, I couldn't bring myself to care at the moment.

When I was finished, I set the tray on the floor and picked up the bulging towel. Opening the bundle, I was ecstatic to discover soap, a razor, a hair comb, a toothbrush, and toothpaste. "Oh, thank you, Jesus," I said out loud, laughing like a maniac. "I'll get to go to my execution looking nice. Thank you. Thank you." *Be thankful to God in all things, right?*

I cleaned myself up over the combination toilet/sink. There was nothing like a good shave followed by combing all the knots out of my hair, brushing my teeth, and taking a bird bath after a week without adequate hygiene. Touching my smooth cheeks, I laughed again. "Just think," I said to no one in particular, "instead of being a baby-faced killer, I'm going to be a baby-faced *killed*. Oh, that's a good one. Somebody put me on *Mekyu & Tityu's Comedy Hour*. That's rich, real rich." My irrational laughter continued for a good deal of time. When the fit subsided, I sat down to pray another fifteen-decade Rosary.

"Please, Mother Mary," I said aloud after reciting the Apostles' Creed, Our Father, three Hail Marys, and the Glory Be, "I'm losing my mind. I don't care what it takes, but give me a chance to live. Any chance, no matter how hard it is. I just don't want to die by violence, especially not when I'm still so young and for a profoundly stupid reason."

A few deep breaths later, and I was able to pray the whole Rosary, meditating on each of the traditional Mysteries (the Joyful, the Sorrowful, and the Glorious) as best as I could from the cold floor of my cell. After that, I just breathed and stared at the wall, letting my mind go blank.

"Human," my cellmate said, or rather gurgled. His voice startled me into sitting up straight.

"Yeah, I'm a human." For whatever reason, I became worried that my cellmate might consider my species delicious. With mouthparts like his, he could make short order of me. It could also explain why he hadn't received a food tray yet. What if the executioner was actually an alien who just ate condemned prisoners? I pressed my hand to my stomach, trying to hold back nausea.

"My name is Henry Trevalu." It would be psychologically more difficult for an alien to devour something with a name, right? Then again, this guy was in maximum security prison. There was no telling what he was capable of. And here I had been whining and ranting at a creature that might be given to interspecies cannibalism, perhaps with a judicial seal of approval. *Oh, Lord Jesus, please get me out of this!*

"I am Alkamor, an Uhumbra." He slid out of his bunk. I stood, not wanting to look like I was cowering in the corner of our cell. Even so, the alien was at least a foot taller than I was, not exactly encouraging. Zakon-4 State Jail certainly had its share of physically imposing inmates, but that was different. That was *jail*. This was *prison*.

"Nice to meet you." A little politeness couldn't hurt. Alkamor curled his tentacle arms in response.

"Likewise," he said, unfurling his tentacles again. "You need not fear me, Henry Trevalu. I am but a humble thief." Alkamor's suckers near the tip of his arm expanded and contracted as though demonstrating his primary means of theft.

"Sticky tentacles instead of sticky fingers?" I said, trying to lighten the mood.

"Precisely." His suckers quit fluctuating, although they continued to vibrate slightly along with the rest of his skin.

"You, uh ... you didn't get the death penalty too, did you?"

"No. I am not a poppy seed dealer like you."

My cheeks heated from the insult. *This thief thinks he's better than me, a victim of circumstance?* "Trevalu Intergalactic Spice Company is a legitimate business. It's not my fault this good-for-nothing planet outlawed one of my family's products the day before I arrived."

"My apologies. I meant no disrespect."

"Yeah, I, um ... It's okay. Sorry I snapped at you. I guess I'm a bit on edge considering I'm going to be executed in a month."

"On edge" was the understatement of the millennium. Try, "totally freaking out inside and being on the verge of a screaming, crying, psychotic break." The thought of my imposed expiration date turned my legs into bouncing liquid, forcing me to sit on the floor yet again. Alkamor slithered close and sat beside me.

"I have lived on Zakon-4 for a long time," he said after a long, painful silence. "I know of only one way to get a death sentence commuted to exile."

My heart leapt with optimism. Those two fifteen-decade Rosaries I prayed were going to pay off after all. "Yeah? What's that?"

"Getting pregnant."

Well, that glimmer of hope lasted about as long as a shooting star. "Sorry, man. I hate to break it to you, but human males can't get pregnant."

Alkamor wriggled his tentacles, seemingly in thought. "I do not understand why you cannot carry young. You have a brood pouch."

"Uh, no, I don't."

"Yes, you do."

What a stubborn, ignorant statement! "Look, man, I've been a human for twenty-two years. If I had a brood pouch, I think I would've noticed it by now."

Alkamor snorted through his nostrils and mouthparts, making a sound somewhere between a frustrated huff and a rumbling fart. "That orifice in the middle of your abdomen. I saw it when you were bathing."

This guy was watching me take a bird bath? I thought he was asleep. And on that note, what a creep! As crowded as the jail was, we at least tried not to stare at each other while using the toilet or taking a shower. "That's not an orifice," I said, a little miffed that I had been watched without realizing it. "It's a belly button."

"Belly button?" Alkamor's mouthparts clicked and his tentacles pulsed. "Explain this belly button and its purpose."

Really? I was a month away from an untimely demise, and my alien cellmate wanted to have a conversation about my belly button? I sighed, too much of a wreck to steer the conversation elsewhere.

"Humans are placental mammals. When we're in utero, we're nourished through an umbilical cord, which is like a feeding tube. Then, when we're born, we don't need the umbilical cord anymore, so we're left with this scar where it used to be attached. That's a belly button. It doesn't have a purpose outside of the womb. It's just there."

Alkamor gurgled, taking in the information. "Ah. Yes, I do remember reading about this. Placental mammals have a navel, also known as a belly button."

"Yeah, so to address your earlier idea, no, I can't get pregnant to avoid execution."

Alkamor's cheeks puffed in and out. "I may be able to assist in helping you obtain a reprieve regardless."

"Yeah? How so?" Did Alkamor have an escape plan? With the force field keeping us inside the cell, getting out of here by brute force didn't seem likely. Of course, I had nothing to lose, so I was up for anything, no matter how outlandish.

"My species can use a host species for gestation."

"Host species?" That wasn't at all what I expected him to say, and I did *not* like where this conversation was going.

"Your navel would make a good point of incision to inject a brood pouch and fill it with my young."

My stomach turned at the thought of slimy, suckered creatures resembling my cellmate crawling around inside of my belly. "Um, are you sure you don't want to pretend to be sick and then overpower the guards to escape?" It sounded stupid the moment I said it, but desperation drove my thoughts.

"Impossible. The only sure way to commute a death sentence on Zakon-4 to exile is if you are pregnant. Serving as a surrogate for my offspring is your only chance."

My breaths shortened due to an extraordinary combination of giddy hope and unfathomable fear. As insane as Alkamor's proposal sounded, it could be my one chance at life that I had prayed so fervently to receive. Insufficient oxygen traveled to my brain, making me a little too amenable to this wild scheme.

"So, uh ..." I cleared my throat, unable to make eye contact. "How exactly do you intend to, um ... do it?"

Alkamor pulled one of his arm tentacles close to his body. Something thin, sharp, and black started to poke through the tentacle's underside. It gradually increased in length until I found myself face to face with something akin to a giant hypodermic needle.

"Is that your, um ... ?" Sweat beaded on my forehead and on the back of my neck. If that thing was going to go inside of me ... A shudder zipped down my spine. Surely there had to be another way to win my appeal.

"There is no exact translation in your language, but in Universal I, it is called a pseudo-ovipositor. I will use it to create a brood pouch inside your abdomen, deposit eggs, and fertilize them."

My eyes traced the length of the pseudo-ovipositor. "Well, hey, man. You've got to be careful with that thing. I've got intestines and stuff in there." I rubbed my stomach. "If you puncture any of my internal organs, I could get an infection and die."

"The penetration will not be deep, only what is sufficient to make an incision."

Penetration? I really didn't like the sound of that. Of course, I didn't like the sound of dying either. "Are you sure there aren't any other loopholes in the law? Anything at all that could get my death sentence overturned?"

"A death sentence for drug trafficking on Zakon-4 has never been overturned except in cases when the defendant was pregnant."

My throat went dry. "Are you absolutely sure of that?"

"I am certain. Pregnancy is your only chance to avoid execution."

This is your moment of decision, Henry, I told myself, taking a deep breath in a pitiful attempt to ease my nerves. *Your fork in the road, your Rubicon. It all comes down to this: do you want to live more than a month, or not?* I swallowed despite my discouraging lack of saliva.

"Do it."

Chapter 8

"Lie flat on your back on the floor."

I did as I was told and lifted my shirt without being asked, exposing my belly button. Despite some misgivings about what I was about to submit myself to, a little ember of hope flickered in my mind. *I'm going to live. Thank you, God. I'm going to live.*

But at what cost? my conscience seemed to say. *Am I doing the right thing?*

"I have no choice but to trust you," I whispered, shushing my doubts. "I want to live."

"You will live. Now, hold still."

Alkamor wrapped one of his tentacles around my middle, holding me in place. My arms and legs remained free, but I was determined not to move. If I could get through two humiliating naked med-scans without flailing – sandwiched between the ceiling and an exam table in full view of stern alien police – then I could get through this.

As Alkamor's pseudo-ovipositor came closer and closer to my belly button, I debated whether or not to close my eyes for the moment of impact. Just as the tip of the needle-like appendage touched my skin, I screwed my eyes shut. It took a lot of self-control not to scream from the incision that followed. My fists and toes clenched of their own accord. This wasn't like getting a shot at the doctor's office; this was fricken' *surgery* without anesthesia.

I opened one eye. Big mistake. The sight of a shiny black weapon that had been driven directly into my belly induced a strangled outcry. Alkamor squeezed my abdomen with his other tentacle, holding me more firmly in place.

"You must not move, Henry Trevalu. Unnecessary movement could cause serious injury."

No kidding. I closed my eyes and willed myself to stay still.

Several seconds later, the pseudo-ovipositor remained lodged in my belly. Just as I was about to ask when Alkamor would remove it, the organ injected a cold, sloppy, gelatinous substance through my navel. Whatever it was expanded within my abdominal wall, making me squirm.

"Hold still. Give the brood pouch a chance to inflate."

Oh, so that's what that slimy thing was. My teeth chattered from fear and disgust, but I forced the rest of my body to remain motionless. Praying a rapid succession of silent Hail Marys kept me from bolting. Once I felt the eggs being deposited – at least, I think those little, hard, round things were eggs – I switched to praying out loud. *Ugh, it feels so gross!* But nothing could have prepared me for the juicy sensation that followed. If I hadn't been crying out to Heaven for mercy, I would have grabbed Alkamor's pseudo-ovipositor by the base and yanked it out of myself, even if doing so caused death. By the grace of God, I managed to lie relatively still until Alkamor withdrew.

"The procedure is complete." Alkamor slithered to the other end of our cell, retracting his pseudo-ovipositor into his tentacle arm as he moved. Blood dripped from my navel.

Procedure? Is that what he calls traumatic insemination? And all because Zakon-4 outlawed poppy seeds the day before I arrived with my shipment.

On the one hand, I should have been glad my Uhumbra cellmate was so clinical. What transpired wasn't lovemaking, just insemination so I would get exiled instead of executed. I had to keep telling myself that. This wasn't sex. It was more like – internal spawning, maybe? On the other hand, the aloofness of the act left me physically and emotionally shaken. Not to mention the sharp sensation from the combination incision and injection from the pseudo-ovipositor directly through my navel.

The floor of our cell felt cold and hard against my back through the thin prison uniform. I sat up, shivering. Something sloshed inside me when I changed positions. At first, it reminded me of how my stomach sometimes rolled like an ocean tide after a hot drink followed by a workout. Only, this time, the interior splashing didn't come from my stomach.

Ugh, alien sperm. A chill zipped down my spine at the realization. Not that I didn't agree to this, but the reality of hosting fertilized alien eggs kicked my anxiety into high gear. Having impregnated me in time for my appeal, Alkamor calmly retreated to the bottom bunk, his red skin and pink suckers pulsating. Apparently, his job was done. I wasn't going to get the equivalent of cuddling or pillow talk, that was for sure. Not that I necessarily *wanted* those things, but still. After several minutes of alien baby making, it all ended so ... suddenly.

The only sure way to commute a death sentence on Zakon-4 to exile is if you are pregnant. Alkamor's words resounded in my brain. *Serving as a surrogate for my offspring is your only chance.*

My mind continued racing through everything that had transpired within the last hour. At first, I didn't want to believe alien impregnation was my only option. I did try to talk my way out of this situation earlier, right? God knows I wouldn't have agreed to surrogacy if there were other viable options. Then again, I *did* pray for a way out of my death sentence, *any* way out. But there should have been some other means of commuting my sentence that didn't involve turning me into a breeding vessel.

Or maybe I should have worked harder on an escape plan. Although in a maximum security prison on a strange alien world, escape would have been impossible. Alkamor said so, and he was right. The guards wouldn't have had any qualms about shooting a dead man walking for making an attempt. After praying two fifteen-decade Rosaries on my fingers, I had hoped a miracle would save me. Instead, I got a belly full of fertilized eggs belonging to a somewhat humanoid, bipedal octopus with big black eyes.

Still sitting on the floor of our cell, I looked down at my stomach. Despite being impregnated only minutes earlier, the injected brood pouch and fertilized eggs formed a bulge behind my navel. The bleeding caused by the pseudo-ovipositor's incision reduced to a trickle, but the sticky sensation of the foreign material lodged in my abdomen remained. At least the sting from the pseudo-ovipositor's injection subsided.

Some good my family's lawyer did, I thought for the hundredth time, tracing the swollen flesh with my fingertips. *If he did his job with an ounce of competence, I wouldn't be in this mess.*

"Henry Trevalu," Alkamor said, bringing my thoughts back to the present. Apparently, he thought it was customary to use a human's full name all the time. Given the extreme stress of my impending execution, I hadn't noticed or bothered to correct him. "Once you are exiled, you must travel to my home world, Uhum, to deliver the young in Tin'volk-uhum, the sea of my origin. The offspring are precocial and will instinctively join a colony of their own kind until maturity."

I nodded, my eyes still focused on my belly. Staring at the little bump raised some uncomfortable questions in my conscience. Had it been a mortal sin to allow an alien to impregnate me, even to save my life? Was this a mockery of God's plan for human procreation? When Alkamor suggested creating a brood pouch within me to circumvent the death penalty, I didn't consider the spiritual or practical repercussions of doing so. Not consciously, anyway. Alkamor's offer was the only way I would continue to survive on a planet eager to destroy me, so I accepted.

My insides gurgled and lurched. Before and during the act, it didn't occur to me to ask how many of my cellmate's offspring I would carry. There must have been quite a few, though, because the "procedure," as he called it, had lasted for several minutes, as far as I could tell. Now that I wasn't in the middle of being impregnated, I visualized the process from beginning to end in alarming detail. Once Alkamor pierced my navel with his pseudo-ovipositor ...

My whole back shuddered and I stifled an outcry, recalling how that sticky substance shot out of Alkamor's needle-like appendage, making a kind of nest in my belly – a brood pouch, he called it. Then, through that same pseudo-ovipositor, he piped in a clutch of tiny eggs followed by a heavy stream of sperm. *Brood pouch, then eggs, then sperm ... Oh, my God, I am so sorry! What have I done? Will You forgive me for letting an alien make babies inside my body?*

"How many babies are there?" I said, stroking the bump. My navel quit bleeding. Would it bleed again when it was time for the Uhumbra to emerge? I mean, they were going to come out the same way they came in, right?

"Usually between five hundred and two thousand."

"Two thousand?" My eyes widened. I stood up, using the wall for support. Already, the pregnancy affected my balance. Considering that my condition was showing only minutes after the fact, what would happen to my body in the coming weeks?

It wasn't like I had a real womb for the pseudo-octopus fry to grow in comfortably. The injected brood pouch felt more like a small, gelatinous blob or bubble squishing against my intestines. There was no way this thing was going to hold all those aliens. "I can't bring two thousand Uhumbra to term," I said, envisioning my internal organs being crushed as the surrogacy progressed. "I'll explode!"

"You will not explode," Alkamor said, still lounging in his bunk. His nonchalant attitude made my skin prickle. This guy may have saved my life, but I had clearly gotten the pump-and-dump treatment – and this from a reproductive act that was about as sexy as going to the dentist. "Newborn Uhumbra are very small. Carrying them within the brood pouch will not pose a problem."

They won't pose a problem? I thought, still clinging to the wall for support. Maybe giving birth to two thousand baby Uhumbra wouldn't kill me, but carrying them would *definitely* pose some problems. Physically, emotionally, socially, religiously – how could a guy in my situation *not* have a myriad of issues after cheating the death penalty by getting knocked up?

"When Uhumbra use a surrogate species, gestation lasts approximately three standard months." Alkamor's tone was eerily detached, as though he was giving a lecture to a group of medical students.

"Three standard months? That means when I have my appeal next month, I'll be – " I cupped my hand in front of myself, miming how freakin' big I'd get by the time I reappeared before the Zakonian Grand Council.

Alkamor cocked his head and swiveled his tentacle arms. His skin rippled. "Yes, you will be quite large. This will be beneficial for obtaining your reprieve."

"Yeah, I guess it will." I managed to step away from the wall. The contents of my brood pouch jiggled a bit but not as dramatically as before. That former feeling of standing on a rocking boat gave way to bubbly popping sensations. I touched the little bump protruding from my navel. It felt warm with activity. Were the Uhumbra already hatching inside of me?

Somehow anticipating my question, Alkamor said, "Within the next twelve standard hours, all of my offspring will hatch inside your brood pouch. The young will eat their discarded egg shells. After that, they will obtain nourishment from you whenever you eat."

I groaned at the thought of all those Uhumbra hatching inside my body, only to grow there for the next three months. Then, I would have to give birth to them. How was I supposed to do that? It was hard enough having them pumped into my belly as tiny eggs, but once they reached their full size? "Please tell me I haven't agreed to a fate worse than death." *Is it weird that I'm more freaked out about hosting and birthing up to two thousand alien life forms than getting executed?*

Alkamor's cheeks inflated and deflated. "I do not understand. You will be exiled, travel to Uhum, give birth in Tin'volk-uhum, and then return to your life. How could this be worse than a premature death at the hands of Zakonian executioners?"

"You don't get it. It's just ... I'm not ... " I started pacing, my chest tightening. "It's just weird, that's all. Look at me! I'm a freak of nature, a mortal sinner, a ... a ... " I clawed at my hair, unable to get a firm grasp on my own thoughts. Pregnant for less than an hour and already experiencing hormonal mood swings? *This is not good.*

"Your distress will pass. Uhumbra surrogacy is often difficult for host species."

"Gee, maybe you should've told me that before getting me pregnant in the first place!" *And maybe I should have thought this through before accepting impregnation in a desperate attempt to avoid the death penalty.*

Alkamor twisted his tentacles while his suckers and skin vibrated. Whether I was hoping he would argue with me or offer comfort, I couldn't say, but his silence elevated my agitation. As I sank to the floor, my throat tightened. Within seconds, a lump formed that I couldn't swallow. I cried.

Chapter 9

In the month leading up to my appeal, I wasn't allowed out of my cell. Condemned prisoners like me didn't have the privilege of going to the mess, yard, or anywhere else. Since I didn't have to share quarters with nearly two dozen prisoners, at least there was room for light exercise in my cell. My muscles had atrophied, no question, but daily stretching and walking built them up a little.

Alkamor didn't know how much physical activity would be safe for a human carrying Uhumbra, so I refrained from sit ups and push ups even though I hated feeling so weak. Instead, I walked in circles while praying a five-decade Rosary on my fingers every morning, prayed the next five decades while walking in the afternoon, and did a third prayer walk in the evening. It helped firm up my legs a little while also displaying some contrition. At night, I said the Angel of God prayer, even though the singsong words sounded childish. Dang it, I was *with* children. Call me a sissy, but imagining my guardian angel's protective wings extending over me and my pregnant belly at night helped.

Hygiene consisted of taking bird baths and shaving over the toilet. I tried to console myself and be grateful that Kalka'ahn Maximum Security State Prison provided me with hygiene items. During my week in Zakon-4 State Jail, I couldn't even brush my teeth. On that note, I ran my tongue over all of my teeth, testing for any possible toothaches. Everything felt fine despite the rough treatment. Hopefully, my pregnancy wouldn't rob nutrients from my body to the point of giving me a cavity. That happened to my mom when she was carrying me.

My meals, if they could be called that, were delivered. The food tasted terrible before, but pregnancy must have heightened my senses, because every bite of that gray, viscous glop made me gag. Even licking up every sticky scrap, as disgusting as it was, left me hungrier than ever. After all, I was eating for approximately two thousand. I begged the guards to increase my rations for the sake of the "little ones," as I'd started calling them, but they ignored me. *Typical.*

Despite the meager portions, my belly continued to grow daily. Within a day of impregnation, the Uhumbra hatched inside my brood pouch. The sensation, although indescribable, was unmistakable. By the end of the first week, the little ones started swimming around inside me, upsetting my stomach. Their growth caused the brood pouch to inflate, pushing it more deeply into my intestines. That meant answering the call of nature more often. Moreover, I couldn't stop touching my expanding middle. It was like an inner compulsion, to caress and pet the bump. Since Uhumbra weren't mammals, my chest remained flat, a small mercy in light of the other physical changes.

Emotionally, I was a mess. Pacing, complaining, weeping, nail biting, hair pulling ... Once, I actually screamed. Alkamor ignored my erratic behavior. That probably wasn't too difficult for him considering we didn't always share quarters. Since his sentence for grand theft didn't carry the death penalty, he enjoyed far more freedom of movement than I did. The guards removed him from our cell frequently for meals and recreation. While I should have been grateful for the periods of solitude, Alkamor's prolonged absences added to my distress. It became surprisingly easy to vilify him, to cast him as the absentee, deadbeat dad in my troubled mind. Well, deadbeat *parent* anyway. As I came to learn a few days after my impregnation, Uhumbra were actually hermaphroditic. In retrospect, I should have known that. After all, how else could I have been impregnated by a single alien creature that produced both eggs and sperm?

Sleep didn't bring any calmness or relief. The bunk's nearly nonexistent mattress induced frequent neck and backaches. It was almost as bad as that communal futon in the Zakon-4 State Jail. Bizarre dreams haunted me every night, dreams of disapproving saints, being shunned by my parents, bleeding to death during delivery, receiving a stay of execution only to be sent to the gallows after giving birth, and – oddly the most terrifying – sitting down to write a list of baby names for two thousand little Uhumbra. As the long nights passed, my strict prayer regimen devolved into incoherent, blubbering pleas to make my suffering stop.

Visitors were prohibited for death row inmates, an especially cruel policy now that I had all of those little aliens rapidly growing inside my manufactured brood pouch. As embarrassing as it was to admit, I wanted my mother. She knew what it was like to have another living creature developing inside her body. Obviously, she was never pregnant with a brood of aliens, but at least her maternal presence and know-how would have bolstered me. If courtrooms on Zakon-4 were open to the public, she would have been there. I tried to remember her expression when I caught a glimpse of her and Dad while being transported to prison, dazed from the verdict. Even that small amount of visual contact had given me some hope.

In contrast, Alkamor didn't provide any emotional support. When I had questions or fears about my surrogacy, he only stated dry facts:

No, it does not matter in which position you sleep as long as you do not sleep on your abdomen. No, you will not need to feed or otherwise care for the offspring after you give birth. I have explained already that they are precocial. No, they do not contain any of your DNA. You are merely a vessel. Yes, your occasional nausea is normal. Yes, your brood pouch is strong enough to hold all of the offspring for the duration of your pregnancy. It moves and expands, but it will not break. Yes, the babies will be expelled out of your navel where the brood pouch is attached.

Day after day, Alkamor responded like this, kicking what remained of my morale into the corner of our pitiful cell. Would it have killed him to say, "You'll be okay, man," just once? I felt like telling him so but held back. What would be the point? Did I really want to hear sweet nothings from a slimy alien who inflicted this misery on me in the first place? Still, the total lack of affection or even understanding brought me back to Zakon-4 State Jail, how I held Traiyo's hand before he would have died from emotional neglect. Of course, Traiyo was a Lularian. His physiology depended upon loving touch as much as air, food, and water. Humans weren't so fragile.

Or are we? I thought as I lay in the bottom bunk. If Alkamor had one redeeming quality, it was that he changed bunks with me so I didn't need to climb in my condition. Even so, that wasn't enough to fulfill my intangible needs. *Can spending so much time without love make a human die too? God help me*, I prayed, tears prickling the corners of my eyes. *I know I've sinned, but I'm sorry, and I need help. I've never felt so alone in my life.*

But oddly enough, I wasn't truly alone. At the end of my prayer, an almost pleasant fuzziness spread under my skin, a great deal of it concentrated in my brood pouch. From a strictly biological standpoint, I was just a host for multiple alien embryos – nothing more. Emotionally, though, something else was going on, something ... hopeful? Cradling my growing baby bump, I said, "We'll get through this, my little ones. God willing, we'll survive."

Chapter 10

The morning of my appeal, two guards yanked me out of the cell while I was still half-asleep, having just dreamed about going to confession to apologize for getting myself into this predicament. As they dragged me down the hall, the little ones sloshed around in my brood pouch. So far, my almost daily nausea hadn't led to vomiting, but this was the closest I'd felt. Thanks to the brood pouch pressing into my intestines, my minuscule dinner from hours ago had already digested and passed, meaning there was nothing to throw up except bile. Small blessings, I supposed. With any luck, I wouldn't lose the bile either.

While the guards led me into court, I blinked sleepers out of my eyes. Mr. Finley sat in the courtroom, looking haggard. He glanced at me and then stared at my bulging middle. After carrying my cellmate's young for a standard month, I looked as though I had swallowed an American football. At this rate, two months from now, I'd look like I had a basketball or watermelon on board – maybe one of each.

"Henry Trevalu," the Zakonian Grand Councilman said, reading from his tablet, "you have been found guilty of transporting poppy seeds, a highly illegal and addictive drug, to Zakon-4, and sentenced to death. How do you plead during this appeal?"

Mr. Finley stared at me, as though expecting me to say something. My throat went dry. Nobody prepped me on what to say during my appeal to get my sentence commuted to exile. Alkamor only told me that pregnant prisoners weren't executed. But what was the protocol for making that declaration in front of the Zakonian Grand Councilman and his minions? That good-for-nothing lawyer my parents hired just stared at my abdomen, slack-jawed. *Oh, Lord Jesus, please help me, quick!*

Flooded with memories of learning about Mary Read and Anne Bonny during a grade school history unit on the Golden Age of Piracy, I blurted out, "I plead my belly!"

The Zakonian Grand Councilman nearly dropped his tablet. "I beg your pardon?"

It felt like I'd swallowed a handful of sand. Still, I forced myself to speak again. This was my last chance. "I'm pregnant." I held up my shirt, even though the bump was visible through the threadbare uniform. Exposed, it looked even more pronounced. The Uhumbra wiggled, probably feeling the subtle change in temperature now that they were no longer covered by a thin layer of fabric.

"Zakonian Grand Councilman and Council," Mr. Finley said, "my client is entitled to have his sentence commuted from execution to exile on account of harboring innocent life, which he must then care for."

Finally, that guy was starting to earn his pay. Adding that line about having to care for my young would provide extra protection. Otherwise, what would stop the Grand Council from allowing me to deliver and then killing me?

"This must be verified." The Zakonian Grand Councilman tapped on his tablet. A long silence followed. I lowered my shirt, having made enough of a spectacle of myself. Covered again, the little ones settled down. Hopefully, they would nap for a while to give me a break from the nausea.

Scooting toward my lawyer, I whispered, "What's going on?"

"I imagine he's calling a doctor to see if your claim is true."

"You *imagine*? Don't you know anything about Zakonian law?" My whole body sweated and tensed. "If you did a better job defending me, I wouldn't have needed to get pregnant to save my hide."

Mr. Finley looked around. "You mean, you're really ... ?" His eyes darted to my bulge.

My indignation came out in a stage whisper. "Of course I'm really pregnant! Did you think this baby bump magically appeared on its own?"

"Well, no, but ... how?"

"How? What difference does it make how? The point is, I'm getting out of here alive because of it." *And I better race to confession afterward for getting myself into this sorry state. Although, will my confession count if I'm not sorry to be alive?*

He shook his head, conveying a combination of discouragement and disbelief. "Your parents will be so disappointed."

Disappointed? So, this guy is judging me now, after doing such a crap job with my initial trial and doing next to nothing for my appeal? I resisted the urge to strangle him, or at least grab him by the lapels to give him a good shake. "Listen, they'd be more disappointed to attend my funeral," I whispered through my teeth.

My stomach growled. Those guards could have served me breakfast before bringing me into court, but no. The little ones squirmed inside my brood pouch again. I could tell they were hungry. Their mouthparts had developed enough to nibble. Instinctively, I stroked my belly, trying to comfort them. "I'm sorry," I said, looking down at the bulge. "We'll eat as soon as this trial's over, okay, little guys?"

"Little guys?" Mr. Finley's voice irritated me. Why didn't he use his big yap for something useful, like defending me properly in court the first time around, instead of interrupting my moment with the little ones? "You mean, there's more than one?"

"Yes," I said, trying not to snap or scowl. "There are between five hundred and two thousand Uhumbra."

Mr. Finley's mouth flapped like a puppet. In all fairness, I probably did the same when I first learned the size of my surrogate brood.

The Zakonian Grand Councilman returned with an old Zakonian woman in his wake. She carried a small medical scanner. Nobody bothered with preambles. The woman just walked over and scanned me. My little brood wriggled, bothered by the intrusion. I petted the bump again, feeling sorry that the med-scan beam entered their space without warning. They were such sensitive creatures.

"The prisoner's claim is true," the woman told the Grand Council. "He is pregnant with multiple life forms."

"I see." The Zakonian Grand Councilman cleared his throat. "Our laws are exceptionally clear. It is both illegal and immoral to destroy innocent life."

Of course, the Zakonian Grand Councilman and Council didn't give a hoot about *my* innocent life before I had two thousand alien babies in the oven, but I wasn't going to argue myself out of a reprieve.

"As the prisoner is himself an alien, we cannot be certain of his offsprings' needs during and after the pregnancy. Therefore, we have no choice but to commute his sentence to exile. Henry Trevalu, you have eighteen standard hours to leave Zakon-4, never to return. If you fail to leave within this time frame or attempt to return, you will be imprisoned until delivery and executed afterwards. This case is closed."

Eighteen hours to get off of this planet modeled after Earth's Dark Ages? That was more than generous. I would be out of here on the first space shuttle to anywhere, forget my confiscated cargo ship. Heck, I hadn't even thought of *Neon Durango* since my arrest, which showed how little it really mattered. And once out of danger, I would seriously consider suing Mr. Finley for his general incompetence during this whole affair.

Before allowing me to leave the courtroom, the Zakonian Grand Councilman ordered that my possessions be returned.

Oh, right. It wasn't like I could've waltzed out of there dressed like a death row inmate. Unsurprisingly, he reiterated that *Neon Durango* and its contents remained impounded because of the poppy seeds. Whatever. That sixteenth birthday present that I once held so dear meant nothing to me now. Ships were replaceable; my life wasn't. At least I would be getting my clothes back in exchange for this cursed prison uniform still stained with the blood from my traumatic insemination. I'd get my watch back too. Not to mention my socks and shoes. Mr. Finley packed up his tablet while we waited, disturbingly calm.

"That was a close call," he said, locking the device into his briefcase. "You got lucky."

Lucky? This stooge thinks I'm lucky to be pregnant with approximately two thousand aliens? I bit back the urge to cuss him out. Why add foul language to that confession I needed to make once I fled from this disgusting excuse for a planet?

"Once you're out of here," Mr. Finley whispered, "I know a guy who can take care of your little problem." He raked his eyes over my belly, his meaning clear.

Was it unchristian to admit how much I wanted to sock this guy? How could he be so matter-of-fact when making that suggestion? My little ones were alive! Forcing my voice to stay low and calm, I said, "I'm not adding another mortal sin to the docket, thank you."

The guards returned with the clothes I had been wearing when I got arrested and directed me to change in the courthouse restroom. A weird policy to be sure, but I wasn't in a position to complain. Also, with all the activity in my brood pouch, I *really* needed to go, despite my empty stomach. If there was one reason to be grateful, it was that I'd been wearing sweats at the time of my arrest. The fabric stretched enough to accommodate and conceal my baby bump. Not that I could hide my condition forever, but if my parents were waiting outside, I'd rather say "hello" before getting the third degree.

Outside of the courtroom, the air smelled fresh. After spending a month in prison, it was like my nose had forgotten cleanliness existed. Now, it remembered. The little ones jumped with happiness. Then again, maybe I just imagined the reason behind their reaction. Either way, Mr. Finley disappeared. He must have slipped out the back. *Good riddance.*

Chapter 11

My parents leaned against the fence surrounding the courthouse, just as they had been when I was first taken to Kalka'ahn Maximum Security State Prison. The guards escorted me as far as the gate and then slammed it behind me. It hadn't finished closing when Mom and Dad seized me in an aggressive hug. Dread overwhelmed me. They were squeezing me too hard, distressing the little ones who began swimming around wildly. I pulled back to protect them, only to feel my face getting kissed and caressed. The little ones settled down, probably feeling safe now that they weren't being squashed.

"You're free," Mom said, still touching my cheek. Dad clamped his hand on my shoulder, like he was afraid to let go. A flurry of pleasantries, questions, and concerns followed: *We're so glad you're safe. Are you holding up okay? Were you fed enough? You've gotten pale. We need to get you to a resort where you can soak up some sun.* Stuff like that. Thanks to the joyful chaos of my release combined with my baggy clothes, my parents failed to notice my distended abdomen.

"Mom, Dad, we've got to get out of here," I said as soon as I could get a word in. "My sentence was commuted to exile. They're giving me eighteen hours to leave or I'm getting executed. And they impounded *Neon Durango*." Maybe I did still feel a little attached to my cargo ship to tack on that little tidbit. But it sure as heck wasn't worth risking execution to attempt to get it back.

"Right, let's move." Dad ushered us into our family ship and flew off planet. Mom cried, so happy to have me back safe and sound. While Dad piloted, Mom dried her tears and gathered our Rosaries to lead a family prayer in gratitude for my release. When I touched the olive wood beads of my Rosary, a sense of safety enveloped me. The warm sensation only lasted for a few seconds, but it was enough to help me realize that things were finally going to be okay.

Then, about half of my alien occupants rolled around in my brood pouch, replacing the warmth with nervousness. Mom initiated the Apostles' Creed, totally unaware of my churning thoughts and stomach. Dad prayed aloud from the cockpit, also oblivious. I mumbled along with the Joyful Mysteries, too distracted by my secret to meditate. Thinking about the Annunciation and the Visitation only reminded me about my own bizarre pregnancy. By the time we reached the Nativity, visions of my impending navel delivery in the Tin'volk-uhum Sea clouded out any thoughts of the miracle of Christ's birth.

Knowing I wouldn't be able to offer a semblance of concentration during the Fourth Joyful Mystery, I instead silently asked God for courage to break the news.

"I have something to tell you," I said when we finished reciting the Rosary. The little ones squirmed. Either that, or my stomach did. "There's a reason why I got my sentence commuted to exile that has nothing to do with Mr. Finley."

"Whatever the reason for your release, I'm grateful," Dad said, switching the ship to autopilot. He came out of the cockpit to sit with us.

"Me too." Mom embraced me. "We're all so blessed to have you back." How could she not feel the bump under my clothes? Was she so relieved by my return that her motherly powers of observation took a vacation? Then again, what human mother would suspect her *son* was pregnant?

"Promise me you won't be angry," I said, twisting out of her grasp. Noticing that my Rosary was still in my hand, I squeezed the Crucifix for fortitude. "And I promise to go to confession as soon as possible."

"Angry?" Dad shook his head. "Whatever the problem is, I'd say you get a pass after everything you've been through."

"What is it, Henry?" Mom said, cupping my cheek. "Whatever it is, we'll figure it out."

"The only way to get a death sentence commuted on Zakon-4 is pregnancy," I said, bracing myself for the fallout. Mom's hand dropped away from my face. Her expression scrunched in consternation, like she couldn't figure out what I was saying.

"Are you telling us you got some Zakonian woman pregnant in order to avoid execution?" If I didn't correct Dad's misconception, he probably would've turned the ship around so I could marry the woman I ruined and take her with us.

"No, it's nothing like that. I'm ... " The word got stuck in my throat. My parents looked at me, glanced at each other, and then focused on me again. My Rosary hung loosely from my hand, not giving me the emotional strength I hoped it would. Still unable to speak, I lifted my sweatshirt with my free hand, revealing the bump. They stared at it, speechless. Miraculously, my voice returned.

"Yeah," I said, swallowing back a lump. "I'm pregnant."

My parents stared with huge eyes and gaping mouths. Mom tentatively placed her hand on my uncovered belly. The little ones jumped beneath the surface, causing Mom to pull back and gasp. She looked at Dad, her lower lip trembling.

"Who did this to you?" Dad's voice took on a sinister tone, his deadly scowl directed at whoever got me in the family way.

"My cellmate," I said, my throat tightening again. Dad clenched his fists. "He didn't force me, though," I said, sensing the reason behind Dad's anger. "I consented because it was the only way to avoid getting executed."

"Oh, honey," Mom said, hugging me and rubbing my back. That lump in my throat dissolved into tears. I wept into Mom's shoulder, just like I wanted to do in prison. Screw stoicism. It wasn't like I was wailing because I stubbed my toe or something. A standard month's worth of fear, pain, humiliation, and all-around trauma flowed out of me in hulking sobs. Mom just held me. Dad remained nearby, not touching me but not acting ashamed of me either. It was the best response I could have possibly hoped and prayed for.

When there were enough breaks in my choking cries to get some words out, I said, "I don't want to go to hell for letting this happen to me to save my skin."

"Don't ever think that," Dad said, his voice calm again. "You did what you needed to do to survive. It's okay." He patted my shoulder in reassurance, calming me. For whatever reason, sometimes a single pat on the back from Dad meant more than all those hugs from Mom. And sometimes, it was the other way around. It made me feel like an overgrown kid, but I guess everyone needs a family's affection sometimes, especially when everything else in life feels like it's on a fast track to hell.

Mom pulled back and squeezed both of my arms. "Don't you worry, honey. We're going to take care of you and the baby. Everything will be all right."

"*Babies.*" I broke eye contact to stare at my bulge. My tears slowed down. "There are supposed to be between five hundred and two thousand of them."

"Two thousand?" my parents said at the same time. Mom rubbed my shoulder, looking toward Dad for support. Dad visibly swallowed, unable to offer any.

"It's not as bad as it sounds," I said, snuffing up my snot. It sucked that I needed to comfort my parents at a time like this, but I didn't really have a choice. "They're Uhumbra, and they're really small at first. My cellmate told me I need to go to his home world, Uhum, and give birth to them in the Tin'volk-uhum Sea. Then, they'll take care of themselves."

"We better change course for Uhum," Mom said to Dad, still rubbing my shoulder. She gave me a half-smile, like she wanted to be brave for her unwed, knocked-up kid even though she was clearly falling apart inside. "Henry, we're going to make sure you get the care you need."

I nodded, feeling both relieved and numb. The little ones slithered, probably exercising their growing tentacles. My brood pouch squished around from their movements, putting pressure on my intestines again. Since I still hadn't eaten breakfast – and I already took care of business at the courthouse – there was nothing to void. That didn't make the sensation any more comfortable.

Dad returned to the cockpit to change course. "We'll need to stop at Planète Bonne Chance first to refuel."

"And I'll need some breakfast. Brunch, actually." Forcing a smile, I said, "After all, I'm eating for about two thousand."

Without hesitation, Mom dug through her pursc and handed me an energy bar. I tore off the wrapper and snarfed it down. "Thanks." Who would've thought granola could be so delicious? While that tided me over, Mom put away our Rosaries and then whipped up some hot rice cereal in the galley. The little ones nipped at my brood pouch, enjoying the energy bar and hungry for more. I lay back and thanked God my parents didn't freak out too much. Actually, they were being unbelievably supportive, which was exactly what I needed after surviving the most horrific month of my life.

"It's going to be okay," I whispered, stroking the little ones through my sweatshirt. "We'll get through this."

Chapter 12

On the way to Planète Bonne Chance, Mom continued fussing over me. To a lesser extent, Dad did too. Even though I was hungry enough to consume half of the galley's contents, Mom made me ease my way back into decent food so I wouldn't make myself sick. After serving me a bowl of hot rice cereal – my first good meal in over a month – she put a pot of homemade chicken soup on the stove. So, in the evening, I had that with some toast. After two healthy but easy to digest meals, the little ones tumbled wildly, behaving as though they were delighted to finally obtain proper nourishment. Their activity warmed my core.

In between eating, light exercise, resting, and reassuring my parents that I'd be okay, I knitted – not because of a burgeoning parental instinct but because it helped combat boredom during the long space flight. About three days of nonstop travel later, I finished knitting a scarf, was well-fed from our supplies, went through several changes of clean clothes, found myself frequently bundled up in a blanket, got comfortably propped up on pillows for plenty of naps, and watched several in-flight movies.

The last full day of our flight, I made an appointment to see a priest in order to make my confession about this surreal situation. Thanks to the church's new online confession scheduling portal, it was quick and easy to schedule everything through my watch. More than that, it saved me the embarrassment of having to speak with a parish office secretary or volunteer about my needs. Not that I would've had to get specific over the phone, but just saying the words, "I'd like to make an appointment for confession" to a third party would have required way more humility than I was currently prepared to exercise. It was an irrational fear, but admitting something like that out loud to a total stranger would've felt too vulnerable – too raw and real. So, thank goodness for technology.

However, trying to line up a doctor specializing in cross-species pregnancies and surrogacies was where I officially lost my nerve. Every time I attempted to place a call, I hung up either right before or right after the receptionist answered. Attempting to set an appointment through the doctor's office's online scheduling portal didn't work out either. For some reason, I just couldn't bring myself to say or type something along the lines of, "Hi, I'm a human male who's pregnant by an Uhumbra."

Dad sat in the reclining chair beside mine while Mom took a turn piloting. Apparently, she didn't trust the autopilot feature to navigate an upcoming rough patch of space. "Not when we have precious cargo on board," she said to me with a wink before taking command. *Cargo, right*, I thought, touching my overgrown middle. *Very funny.*

"Hey, Dad?" I said when it looked like he might start channel surfing or reading a digital newspaper on his watch.

"Yeah?"

"Um, I wasn't able to make a doctor's appointment." That sounded incredibly juvenile when stated aloud, but there it was.

"Why? Is there a connection problem? You can try my watch or the ship's television if your watch isn't working."

"No, it isn't that. There's nothing wrong with my watch. It's just ... " I ran my hand through my hair, stressed and stalling for time. Man, after more than a month of captivity, I needed to see a barber too.

"Well," I said, looking at my hands. My nails were alternately too long or bitten and chipped. *Wow, better add an appointment with a manicurist. And who knows what my feet and toenails look like after a month of being barefoot on hard prison floors? I'll need a pedicure too.*

"I keep chickening out." *There! I said it.* "Sorry, I'm being such a wuss that I can't even make my own doctor's appointment."

"You're not a wuss, Henry."

I don't know why I expected him to tell me to man up and make the call. That wasn't really Dad's style, so it shouldn't have surprised me that he was being so nice about my shortcomings. But I thought he would at least give me a pep talk or something.

The more I thought about it, the less rational it was to avoid making an appointment, especially when my life might depend upon it. After all, I'd been pregnant for a month without prenatal care in a gestation estimated to last only three months. Technically, I was entering my second trimester.

"Never mind," I said. "I'll get it done." I tried to set a date online but fumbled with my watch and dropped it. Bending down to retrieve it proved nearly impossible with my oversized gut in the way. Dad leaned over and picked it up for me.

"Don't worry about it," he said, still holding on to my watch. "I'll make your appointment."

"It's okay, Dad. I'll get a grip. You don't have to – "

He waved me off. "Consider it pregnancy privileges. You've got enough to deal with right now." Dad squeezed my shoulder on the way out of the room. "Just rest."

Rest? I groaned. Practically all I had been doing around here was resting. I needed to stand up and stretch. That is, if I could get up from the reclining chair unassisted. The basketball-sized abdominal mass wreaked havoc on my center of gravity. Even with the chair pushed upright, it took some effort to get out of it, but I managed.

Standing on the salon deck gave me a twinge in my back. At first, I thought it was just soreness from sitting too long, but the feeling didn't go away. Come to think of it, my little ones became awfully still all of a sudden. *Oh, crap. Something's wrong!*

"Mom!" I hurried to the cockpit, trying to maintain my balance despite the increasing space turbulence.

"Henry, sit down and buckle up. This is a difficult area to navigate and the turbulence is going to get worse."

I strapped myself into the co-pilot's chair. "Mom, I think something's wrong. My back hurts, and the babies ... "

The little ones swirled inside me. Despite their churning inducing a light bout of nausea, I couldn't have been more elated. I sighed and put my hand on my belly. "They're still moving. Thank you, God," I said, tilting my head toward the ceiling in gratitude. "I guess they were just asleep." The Uhumbra did that sometimes, but with my sudden back pain, I forgot and panicked. "Don't scare me like that," I said to my brood. They merely bumped about in that carefree way of theirs.

Mom concentrated while she steered to avoid the worst of the turbulence. It passed within a couple of minutes. As soon as it was safe, I removed my safety belt to reduce the pressure on my body.

"You said your back is sore?"

"Yeah," I said. "It's not a sharp pain, but it's there."

"Well, I don't know much about Uhumbra surrogacy, but I do know that I got a sore back sometimes when you were on board. It makes sense, you know. It's like you've got a melon strapped to your middle." She laid her palm on my belly, as though I needed a physical reminder of how big I had gotten. "That adds extra weight up front that can be hard on your back." Mom pulled her hand away. "Just be sure to tell the doctor. In the meantime, a hot water bottle or disposable heat pad might help."

"Thanks. I'll get a heat pad from the lav." Gripping the arms of the co-pilot's chair, I hoisted myself to my feet. On the way to the lav, I became overwhelmed by an inexplicable urge to drink a glass of milk. So, I made a detour to the galley. The blueberry muffins Dad made last night looked pretty tempting too, so I helped myself to one.

"I am perturbed that I have been on hold for so long," I overheard Dad say in his and Mom's cabin. "This is unacceptable for a clinic. Suppose someone were seriously ill or injured and needed to contact you urgently?"

While enjoying my muffin and milk, I lingered in the hallway to eavesdrop, trying not to spill or make crumbs.

"Yes, well, I'm afraid I'll be contacting a different clinic and suggest you update your protocols to reduce hold times." It sounded like Dad hung up. That didn't surprise me in the least. One of Dad's hot button issues was any company with phone trees, automated phone systems, and/or excessive hold times. He prided himself that Trevalu Intergalactic Spice Company held the highest industry standard when it came to customer service. A real, live, competent, polite person always answered the phone in a timely fashion and handled issues promptly.

Oh, man ... It felt like someone slammed a crowbar into my back. Gritting my teeth, I made my way to the lav to get that heat pad. Mom would've had a fit if she knew I set down my milk and muffin on the lav's counter, calling it "unsanitary."

Although after spending a week in Zakon-4 State Jail abutted by twenty-some guys' personal filth, setting a half-eaten muffin next to a bathroom sink was nothing.

Squatting to reach the box of adhesive heat pads stored in the cabinet under the sink wasn't a problem; trying to get back on my feet afterwards was the problem. *Okay, Henry, take it one step at a time.* I eased myself onto my butt and stuck one of the air activated heat pads on my lower back. It would take a few minutes to warm up, but at least it would provide a safe means of pain relief. Now, I just needed to figure out how to stand up. *Ah, I'll use the toilet for leverage.*

Scooting around on the lav floor reminded me of the Elbaren who had to galumph around the floor of our cell in Zakon-4 State Jail on account of lacking humanoid legs. To think that the poor guy had to do this all the time in the absence of water to swim in. No wonder he splashed about happily during those chain gang shower times. It would have been the one brief time of the day where he felt somewhat normal.

I grabbed the edge of the toilet seat with both hands and tucked my knees under myself. Now came the hard part – actually standing. *Okay, one, two, three!* After straining to lift upward – with a sore back, no less – I needed to take a break. *Ah, thank goodness I have a throne to sit on.*

Not a moment too soon either. The little ones took a notion to move inward rather than outward, pressing into my intestines again. *Well,* I thought while emitting a cross between a groan and a sigh, *at least I'm already in the lav.*

After cleaning up, I took my milk and half-eaten muffin with me. Padding down the hall with my snack, I overheard Dad on the phone again and stopped to listen.

"Yes, that's correct," he said. "My son's human, and he's pregnant ... I beg your pardon? ... No, this is *not* a practical joke. What kind of intergalactic clinic are you running anyway to ask a question like that?" There was a long pause followed by Dad muttering to himself. He must have hung up again. I didn't catch all of his private rant, but it sounded like he was agreeing with whoever said that stupidity, not hydrogen, was the most common element in the universe.

Maybe it was time for me to step in. Fortified with a snack and a heat pad, I felt better able to handle the phone call that was getting Dad more worked up than I was. I knocked on his door.

"Come in."

"Dad, I, uh ... I was just wondering how things were going with the doctor's appointment."

"Awful! I'm running out of clinics to contact on Planète Bonne Chance that aren't full of idiots and losers. The last clinic I called thought that my trying to line up a prenatal care appointment for you was a practical joke." He tightened his lips, clearly not amused.

"Well, in all fairness, Dad, wouldn't you think the same if you were running a medical clinic and some human called to report that his *son* was pregnant? I mean, it doesn't really make sense unless it were a joke."

Dad sighed. "Yeah, I guess."

"How about if I make my own appointment?" I said, reaching for my watch. "I know I punked out earlier, but your blueberry muffin has enough sugar to power me through this."

"Oh, are you saying I used too much sugar?" Dad said, feigning offense.

"No, I'm saying you used just enough sugar to make me forget how embarrassed I should be to make that phone call." I took my watch back from Dad, grinning. "Thanks for trying to get things lined up, though."

"You're welcome, although I'm the one who's embarrassed right now. Here I'm running an intergalactic spice company, and I can't manage to get you prenatal care without losing my cool or making people think it's a prank call."

"It's okay, really. I'll take care of it."

I returned to my cabin, feeling kind of sorry for Dad. Yeah, I was the one going through all this crap, but it had to be killing him to see his son in the family way and not being able to do anything about it.

All right, Henry, you can do this, I told myself as I sat on the edge of my bed. *And St. Gabriel, you're the patron saint of telephones, right? Well, wish me luck.*

Chapter 13

"Planète Bonne Chance Clinic 24," a woman said on the other side of the phone call. "This is Yolanda speaking. How may I help you?"

"Yes, I, um ... " I cleared my throat. "I'm Henry Trevalu, and I read on your website earlier that you specialize in cross-species pregnancies and surrogacies?"

"Yes, that's correct. Do you need to schedule an appointment?"

Wow. Was it really going to be this easy? Thank you, St. Gabriel! "Yes, I do."

"Okay, great. And who is the patient?"

"That would be me," I said, rubbing the back of my neck. "I promise this isn't a prank call; I really am pregnant."

"No worries. Could you please tell me your name again?"

"Henry Trevalu."

"Oh, like Trevalu Intergalactic Spice Company?"

"Yeah, same spelling." I didn't want to confirm my identity as sole heir to the family business. That would just turn an already awkward situation into an oh-my-gosh-I'm-talking-to-a-semi-celebrity thing.

"Got it. Are you ready to schedule?"

"I am. Can you send a virtual calendar to my watch so I can choose a time and date?"

"Sure. Stand by."

A holographic calendar from the clinic hovered above my watch. It automatically overlaid itself on my calendar to prevent scheduling conflicts. I enlarged the layered calendar with a flick of my fingers. It looked like there were plenty of openings, so I tapped the afternoon slot for the next day. That would still leave me plenty of time to complete my morning confession with Fr. Blaise.

"Okay, you're in the system," Yolanda said when I tapped the date. The calendar disappeared on my end. "Just so Dr. Lambert is prepared, do you have time to answer a few questions to help get ready for your appointment? If you'd rather wait to speak with the doctor, that's okay too."

"No, that's all right. You can ask questions." As long as I was on the phone with a nice receptionist, I might as well give any information I could to make my upcoming appointment go more smoothly. "Go ahead."

"All right. First question: you are human, correct?"

"Right. And yeah, I'm a biological male. It's ... kind of a long story."

"That's all right. Are you pregnant with a hybrid fetus, or is this a surrogacy?"

"It's a surrogacy. I'm carrying between five hundred and two thousand Uhumbra."

If Yolanda found that declaration surprising, her voice didn't betray it. "Uh huh. And how long have you been pregnant?"

"About a standard month now, and I know that Uhumbra surrogacies last about three standard months." At least, that was what Alkamor told me. I didn't bother doing any research on the internet or in my digital copy of *Professor Prendergast's Intergalactic Travel Guide*. Things had just been too ... well, *abnormal* around here.

I heard the sound of typing in the background. "Do you have any medical records you can transfer to Dr. Lambert before your appointment?"

"You mean, like, regular doctor records?"

"Yes, a medical history can be helpful, but do you have any records related to your prenatal care until this point?"

A pit formed in my stomach, and not from the little ones scurrying about inside me. Seriously, it felt like they were playing tag in there. "I haven't had any prenatal care." I braced myself, waiting to get scolded for being neglectful or some darn thing.

"Oh, okay. We'll get you taken care of when you arrive, then."

"Thanks. Is there anything else?"

"Nope. Everything's all set. Do you have any questions?"

"No questions, but thanks for being so professional about my needs. Things have been ... tough."

"Of course. And don't worry, Henry. Dr. Lambert will take good care of you."

After a few more pleasantries, we signed off. I returned to the salon and told Mom and Dad about my appointment. Autopilot navigated the ship.

"Planète Bonne Chance Clinic 24?" Mom pursed her lips. "I haven't heard of that one. Are you sure it's legitimate? The last thing you need is to go to some ham-and-egger."

Some "ham-and-egger?" Really? "It's a well-regarded clinic, see?" I projected the website and its reviews above my watch where she and Dad could look it over. "They have good ratings. I'll be fine."

Mom scrolled through the information. "It looks new and clean." Dad enlarged some of the pictures.

"Yeah, it just opened last year. Dr. Lambert is supposed to be really good with cross-species surrogacies. I'll be *fine.*" I wasn't sure if I was saying that to assure my parents or myself, maybe both. Either way, I felt better knowing that I would finally receive medical care.

A ship's alert dinged. "Please fasten your seatbelts," the ship announced. "We are beginning our descent to Planète Bonne Chance and should arrive in thirty standard minutes." Dad went to the cockpit to monitor the landing. I took his place beside Mom in the salon.

Since we had a half hour, we flicked on the television to watch some news. There was a segment about the Earth Embassy of Zakon-4 issuing a report condemning the planet's punitive justice system, continued use of the death penalty for drug offenses, and appalling prison conditions. My apparently high-profile court case came up as an instigating factor for the embassy's official investigation. As the newscaster described the findings of the report – findings I actually lived through – I started feeling a bit queasy. Putting my hand on my belly didn't help, although it did attract the little ones to the heat of my hand. They swarmed toward my belly button, relieving the pressure they had been exerting on my intestines.

"Henry," Mom said, tapping my arm to get my attention. "We can watch something else if you want."

I nodded, so Mom switched to an episode of the game show *Intergalactic Shopper*. During the last commercial break, our ship landed.

Disembarking after almost four days of space travel with my gut growing a little bigger each day threw off my balance more than I anticipated. The transition between space and land didn't usually bother me this much. But this time, I tripped halfway down our ship's ladder, plowing face-first into Mom. Dad grabbed my shoulder from behind, and Mom nearly twisted her ankle on the second to last step by the looks of it. Even with her foot at an awkward angle, Mom refused to let go of the railing, absorbing the blow from my fall. The little ones startled, scattering in every direction inside, but they didn't seem hurt.

"Oh, honey, be careful." Mom sounded way more worried than upset.

"I'm sorry," I said, pulling back from Mom. "Are you okay?" The last thing she needed was a broken foot from my clumsiness.

"Yes, I'm fine," Mom said, "but never mind about me. I don't want you to fall and suffer a miscarriage."

Her concern warmed me. "I promise I'll be more careful."

"At least you're visiting Dr. Lambert tomorrow. Be sure to tell her about your accident, and get a med-scan to make sure everything's okay."

I tried not to roll my eyes. The way she was carrying on, you would think that I fell right on my belly onto hard ground or something. Limping, Mom helped me down the rest of the stairs. Dad maintained his grip on the back of my T-shirt. When we were on solid ground, my parents finally let go of me but hovered as though expecting me to make another crash landing. A few steps later, their concern was no longer warranted – my land legs were coming back pretty fast and the little ones settled down in the brood pouch. Nonetheless, I said a silent prayer of thanks that Mom broke my fall, and that she didn't get injured doing it.

Chapter 14

Planète Bonne Chance was a common pit stop in this sector of the galaxy, so my parents and I had visited lots of times. Le Quartier Humain – established by French explorers, of course – had a sizeable permanent human population as well as travel accommodations for all species. It also boasted one of the planet's few Catholic communities, anchored by St. Joseph Cupertino Cathedral. There was also St. James Catholic Church near the edge of town. Mom preferred it to the cathedral because of its small-town charm, which was the same reason Dad couldn't stand it. Small-town charm, after all, went hand-in-hand with small-town gossip.

I definitely noticed that stuck-up attitude when we arrived for my scheduled confession at St. James the next morning. No longer wearing my sweats, my pregnancy showed. In the almost five days since my appeal, my belly expanded well beyond the point of concealment. Even a day or two before, I could have passed for a guy who enjoyed beer and hamburgers too much. Now, there was no mistaking the reason for my largeness, especially with every other part of me being so thin. Plus, I obviously didn't have maternity clothes on board, so my gut stuck out from under the fabric, showing off its full roundness.

As I made my way toward the confessional, the parishioners' judgmental stares bored into me. Clearly, they saw a pregnant human male as an abomination. Okay, so not all of them acted like a bunch of Pharisees, but enough of them did that I felt sensitive to it. At least scheduling an appointment in advance ensured there wouldn't be a line to talk to Fr. Blaise.

Inside the confessional, I almost used the kneeler but thought better of it. After having trouble getting up from the lav floor yesterday, I didn't want to get stuck on my knees, forcing Fr. Blaise to rush to my assistance at the end of my confession. That would've been the embarrassment of the century. So, I sat down on the chair provided for the benefit of the handicapped. Pregnancy definitely excused me from having to use the kneeler, no sense of guilt here.

"Bless me, Father, for I have sinned. It has been three standard months since my last confession. These are my sins."

I took a deep breath and made an effort to keep my hands folded rather than touching my swollen belly. "I was unjustly imprisoned on Zakon-4, so I allowed myself to be impregnated by an alien in order to get my death sentence overturned."

"Mm hmm."

My breath hitched. While I appreciated that Fr. Blaise was following standard procedure for confessions these days – mostly listening and making occasional noises of acknowledgment – verbally reliving the past created a knot at the base of my throat.

"And I confess the sin of surrogacy, because I allowed an alien to alter my body and lay eggs in it. That's how I'm pregnant now."

"Mm hmm."

"And ... while I was in jail, I claimed all of the prisoners' abandoned food scraps for my own because I was hungry." I wasn't sure if that out-of-context statement made sense to Fr. Blaise, but Jesus knew what I meant, and that was what mattered.

"Mm hmm."

"And I've been harboring hateful feelings toward my lawyer because he did such a bad job defending me. In my heart, I've blamed him for letting myself get pregnant."

"Mm hmm."

"And Father, I'm ... I feel guilty that I'm glad about cheating the death penalty. I mean, I didn't want to die ... " That's when the knot in my throat burst. Normally, going to confession didn't bring me to tears, but my hormones must have been out of whack. That, and maybe I was just plain hitting a breaking point. In between sobs, I said, "I was scared. Should I have accepted death? I mean, I just can't feel sorry for being alive. I can't!"

Fr. Blaise finally spoke. "We never have to feel guilty about being alive."

That simple statement helped a lot. Wiping my face on my sleeve, I concluded, "For these and all the sins I can't remember, I'm heartily sorry."

What transpired next passed through my brain in a soupy blur. The priest absolved me, saying something about how fear of my impending execution must have compromised my state of mind, leading me to accept traumatic insemination by an alien. Of course, surrogacy still constituted a mortal sin as it was divorced from the natural conjugal act reserved for a husband and his wife, and so forth. However, the state of pregnancy itself didn't constitute a sin; that was just a biological condition. After that, he read something from the Bible, but I immediately forgot what it was. At some point, I had to say the Act of Contrition. Thankfully, it was posted in the confessional because I could never seem to remember the words.

Back in the nave, I tried to collect myself. In my effort to stop crying, I forgot that kneeling might make it hard to get up. Too late, I was on my knees for my penance of an Our Father and three Hail Marys. When I finished, an elderly woman sitting in the same pew had to help me to my feet because my belly weighed me down.

"Thanks," I whispered. She smiled and held on to my elbow as I waddled toward the exit. When she returned to church, I said a silent prayer for her health and happiness because she didn't know a thing about how I wound up preggers but exercised true Christian charity regardless.

My parents were waiting for me outside in the church parking lot, ready to drive me to-Planète Bonne Chance Clinic 24 in their rented car. Of course, halfway to my doctor's appointment, we had to stop at a fuel station so I could relieve myself. The little ones pressed into my intestines constantly now, jiggling and jockeying for position. Dad bought snacks for the road so the fuel station owner would let me use the toilet.

Back in the car, I ate the cheese puffs he bought. The little ones wriggled in anticipation of good, old-fashioned junk food. When I finished eating, I stroked my belly. Forgetting that I wasn't alone, I talked to them. Whatever I said to them wasn't anything important, probably something inane like, "Cheese puffs really are tasty, aren't they?" Hearing Dad change the radio station snapped me back into reality.

"Sorry," I said. My cheeks felt warm all of a sudden. Since when did I blush? "I was just ... well, you know."

"There's nothing to be sorry about," Mom said, nibbling on cheese puffs. She handed me some of hers, knowing I was ravenous. "I talked to you when you were in the oven all the time. I sang too."

While I didn't think I would sing to the little ones anytime soon, Mom's response to my behavior helped me relax. At least what I had been doing wasn't certifiably weird. My face still felt warm, though, as did the rest of me. I fanned myself with the Uhum travel brochure that I picked up at the fuel station. No wonder they called pregnancy "in the oven."

When we arrived at Planète Bonne Chance Clinic 24, Mom and Dad sat in the waiting room. Even though I didn't say anything to them on account of filling out digital paperwork, their mere presence provided much needed moral support. The little ones seemed to agree, rocking back and forth inside me in a gentle motion.

A nurse led me into Dr. Lambert's office, subjected me to a battery of health questions, invited me to sit on the exam table, and then left the room to make me wait some more. After a few minutes, the doorknob stirred and the doctor let herself in.

"Hi, I'm Dr. Lambert."

"Henry Trevalu. It's nice to meet you. I'd stand up to shake your hand, but ... " I indicated toward my belly. It looked even bigger than when I went to confession, but maybe that was just an illusion caused by the exam room's lighting.

"That's okay, Henry." She washed her hands and then sat across from me on one of those rolling chairs doctors seemed to favor. "So, I read your intake form and understand that you are a surrogate for between five hundred and two thousand Uhumbra. Is that correct?"

"Yes. I ... It's complicated. The short version is that I got pregnant in prison to avoid a death sentence. So, I haven't been able to access prenatal care until now."

Dr. Lambert nodded. "Okay, then. Let's take a look." She brought out a portable med-scanner. "Ready?"

"Yeah. Go for it."

Dr. Lambert performed the scan, making the Uhumbra leap inside of me. As soon as the beam retracted, I petted my belly to calm the little ones down. It didn't occur to me until later, but the med-scan didn't trigger any horrifying memories of the invasive intake procedures I endured on Zakon-4. Maybe the fact Dr. Lambert used a small device with my permission rather than a full body med-scan allowed my mind to separate medical abuse from compassionate medical care. If I were super traumatized, I might have freaked out anyway. So, at least I was holding myself together *somewhat*, even if it didn't always feel that way.

"Everything looks normal and healthy."

"That's good." What else was I supposed to say?

"And in case you were wondering, the scan has picked up approximately two thousand Uhumbra. It's hard to get an exact number, but you are on the higher end of the spectrum in terms of birth number."

"Oh, joy." Apparently, Alkamor wanted to make sure I was really good and pregnant for my appeal.

"But you should do just fine when it comes time to deliver," Dr. Lambert said with an encouraging smile. "Even so, do you have any questions or concerns?"

Like Mom insisted at least ten times, I told her about how I tumbled down the ladder when disembarking yesterday. It was more of a stumble, really, but it was one of those stories bound to get bigger and bigger with each retelling. I also told her about my recurring episodes of back pain. Dr. Lambert performed an extra med-scan as a precaution. The little ones rebelled at the intrusion by bumping against my intestines.

"No harm done," Dr. Lambert said, reading the second med-scan's results. "Although an actual fall could lead to a miscarriage if you're not careful."

"Right, I'll be more careful on stairs," I said. "Actually, mobility in general has been getting difficult. Like, getting up from a chair and stuff has been brutal."

"That's definitely to be expected with the way your weight is being distributed due to the pregnancy. And since you're male, your center of gravity is going to cause more problems for you than in a typical female pregnancy. You see, in humans, women have a lower center of gravity than men, which is helpful for maintaining balance during pregnancy. So, you have a definite disadvantage in that regard. It means you'll have to be a lot more careful not to fall."

"Thanks for the heads-up."

"As for your back pain, that's pretty normal too. I noticed from the med-scans that you're wearing a disposable heat pad on your back. That's a good, safe treatment option. You can keep doing that as needed. And speaking of treatments, I'm going to write you a prescription for some prenatal vitamins, just to be on the safe side."

"Okay."

After scribbling out a prescription and tapping it to my watch, Dr. Lambert reiterated what Alkamor told me in prison: I needed to give birth on Uhum in the Tin'volk-uhum Sea.

Based on the initial med-scan and simple mathematics, my delivery date was about a month and a half away. I couldn't help gaping at my midsection.

"You're sure I won't pop before then?" I said, wondering how much more expansion my body could endure. At this point, my belly resembled a human woman in her seventh or eighth month of pregnancy – with triplets.

"If it makes you feel any better, you're almost at maximum size," Dr. Lambert said. "Uhumbra growth in a host's brood pouch stops at around two standard months. In the last month of surrogacy, Uhumbra continue to develop internally but don't grow again externally until after they're born."

I sighed with relief. *Thank you, God.*

"In the meantime, you need to travel to Uhum within the next standard week to ensure you'll arrive in time. Depending on traffic and space conditions, the trip can take one to two weeks." Dr. Lambert pulled up something on her watch and touched it to mine to transfer data. "Here, I've uploaded the names and addresses of reputable doctors on Uhum who can help you. I recommend having both a human and an Uhumbra involved in your care and delivery."

"Thanks. I'll do that."

"I've also uploaded dietary information. I know it's hard to eat well on the road, but you can't keep loading up on junk food."

Apparently, all those digested cheese puffs must've shown up on the med-scan, or their chemical compounds did anyway.

Never mind that Mom, Dad, and I ate well on our ship; I didn't want to argue. "I'll try to do better." Dr. Lambert helped me down from the exam table. "Thanks again."

"You're welcome." As I turned to leave, Dr. Lambert said, "By the way, I also took the liberty of uploading the addresses of some shops on Uhum where you can find clothes that might fit you better. While I think it's safe to assume you won't get pregnant again, surrogacy clothing might help you feel more comfortable for the next month and a half."

I looked down at my bare midriff and low-riding pants hooked painfully tight under the baby bump. Yeah, I definitely needed something with more flexibility. "Thanks."

On the way back to the car, my parents bombarded me with questions. I answered them in a fog as we drove to the pharmacy to pick up my prenatal vitamins. This whole pregnancy thing was still pretty overwhelming. While waiting in line at the drive-thru pharmacy, I assured Mom that the med-scans came up normal, and she finally quit ruminating about my misstep on the ship's ladder. Although learning that my balance might worsen because of my high center of gravity gave her another reason to worry. *Me and my big mouth.* Dad rolled his eyes about Dr. Lambert's admonition about not eating junk food on the road but promised not to buy me any more cheese puffs until after I gave birth. They agreed to start the journey to Uhum the next day.

"But tonight," Dad said with a grin, "we're celebrating a good confession and good doctor's report with a nice dinner at the Hôtel Mot-Valise. Dr. Lambert can't complain about your eating five-star cuisine."

"Um, Dad? As much as I like the idea of five-star cuisine, I think the *maître d'hôtel* is going to take one look at me and say 'no shirt, no service.'"

"If we spend enough money, they'll overlook anything. Besides, your sweats should keep you covered up until we buy those surrogate clothes on Uhum, right?"

"Oh, honey, Henry can't wear sweats in a five-star restaurant." Mom pulled up something on her watch. "Here, I found a maternity store only a few blocks from here." She uploaded the directions to the rental car's GPS. "Maybe they'll have some plain shirts and pants that look unisex."

A maternity store? It was awful enough that I needed to go to a surrogacy store when we got to Uhum, but an actual *maternity* store? Like for pregnant *women*? No, I had to draw the line somewhere. I couldn't be seen in public buying women's clothes for myself! "Well, um, you could go in and buy something, Mom. Dad and I can wait in the car."

"Henry, you'll have to go in to make sure you find something that fits."

"Mom, it's a *maternity* store! I can't go in there. Dad, help me out here."

Dad sighed. "Don't drag me into this argument, please."

Thanks a lot.

When Dad parked, Mom drummed her fingers on the dashboard and gave me an unnerving, motherly, I-mean-business stare, waiting for me to comply. Sighing, I got out of the car and followed her inside the store.

"Welcome!" a bubbly clerk said. "May I help you?"

"Hi," I said, trying to be polite. Mom abandoned me at the counter to look through racks of maternity shirts. "Um, as you can see, I'm kind of popping out of my clothes here."

She nodded in understanding. "No worries. Would you like some help finding anything?"

"Yeah, uh ... " I scratched the back of my neck, finding it difficult to make eye contact. "I just need some shirts and pants that don't look too ... well, girly, I guess. No offense."

"None taken. Come with me."

With enthusiastic help from the clerk and my mom, I picked out three pairs of pants and shirts – all in dark, solid colors – and two pairs of maternity pajamas. Surprisingly, the shop had a single stall, unisex changing room, so I was able to make sure they all fit and could wear one of the outfits right away. Loath as I was to admit it, I felt way more comfortable dressed in shirts and pants that accommodated the drastic changes in my body.

"Now," Mom said as we got into the car. Dad had been reading something projected over his watch and closed it when he saw us coming. "Don't you think Henry looks better for dinner at the Hôtel Mot-Valise?"

"Well, I'm not one for fashion, but I have to admit that it does look less ... sloppy."

"Um, thanks?" I said. Never mind that Dad had been the one to insist I could have eaten at a five-star restaurant in my sweats.

Whatever. At least now I didn't feel like my clothes were trying to strangle my guts.

"All right," Dad said, driving off. "Now that we have that settled, it's time for that celebratory dinner. While you were shopping, I read their menu. Go ahead and look while I'm driving. I sent it to both of your watches."

Mom and I pulled up the menu on our watches. My mouth watered at the thought of fine dining. I hadn't eaten in a nice restaurant – *any* restaurant – in months. The little ones must have sensed my anticipation, because they tickled my insides as though begging for their first gourmet meal. *Classic Earth cuisine made with all organic ingredients? I am so there.*

What sounded good in theory turned out to be a disaster. The imported fettuccini with pink sauce, scallops, and peas was delicious but too rich in my condition. While waiting for dessert, the little ones decided to play rough in the brood pouch, ramming my intestines repeatedly. At first, a bathroom break took care of the problem, but after the first bite of vanilla bean ice cream, my guts rebelled. My dinner started digesting in reverse, and there wasn't time to return to the restroom to expel it. Since this wasn't a roadside diner, there weren't any garbage cans nearby. I made it as far as the five-star lobby's beautiful linoleum white floor before puking my guts out.

"S ... sorry."

Hotel staff scurried about, making phone calls and distracting other guests from the mess. One alien guest shrieked at the receptionist, saying the incident left him unclean to perform some sort of religious ceremony. In the commotion, my parents whisked me back to our hotel room. Dad ordered an electrolyte fluid replacement solution from room service. Mom gave it to me in bed. The affronted alien's curses and incantations resounded in my brain while I drank. It was good we were checking out in the morning. There was no way I could live this down.

Chapter 15

If it weren't for my pregnancy, the month my parents and I spent on Uhum would have been like a resort vacation. Watching all of those Uhumbra alternately walk and slither about definitely took some getting used to, but the atmosphere was mostly pleasant – rather tropical in climate and culture. The food was surprisingly nutritious, tasty, and easy to digest, so I didn't repeat my mortifying puking-in-the-hotel-lobby experience. There were also a lot of on-site services, so I was finally able to get a haircut, manicure, and pedicure. A massage was out of the question until after delivery, but that would be something to look forward to. Despite everything that had happened to me, I was looking and feeling pretty good – the best I had felt since before my arrest on Zakon-4, actually.

Mom, Dad, and I tried to keep things as normal as possible, managing Trevalu Intergalactic Spice Company remotely. Also, Dad fired Mr. Finley during a rather irate phone call that was far more satisfying than a Christian should have admitted. Mentioning Mr. Finley's proposal to have my pregnancy problem "taken care of" probably had something to do with it. That, and it kind of was his fault that I got knocked up in the first place for not defending me properly in court. I know I confessed my unfriendly feelings toward him and vowed to do better, but what could I say? I wasn't quite ready to be a saint ...

Another indication of my lack of sainthood? When getting up to go to the bathroom one night, I overheard my parents talking about me from their room. Of course, I stopped to eavesdrop. It was a bad habit from childhood that I never overcame and wasn't sure if I ever would. For whatever reason, even at twenty-two years old, I guess I wanted to know what my parents were really thinking and saying about me when they thought I couldn't hear.

"I know I've said it before," Mom said, "but I'm worried about Henry."

Dad's reply was muffled.

"Yes, I know, but ... the fact that he has two thousand alien creatures in his belly? Oh, my poor baby!" After that, it sounded like she was crying. *Poor Mom. Maybe I shouldn't have stopped to listen in ...*

"Henry's going to be okay. We're here for him."

I decided to stop listening there, not just because I wanted to end my eavesdropping on a positive note but because nature called – and refused to wait.

Just as Dr. Lambert assured me, my belly stopped expanding by the second month, but the little ones continued to develop. Dr. Hollis and Dr. Nakurahan, a human and an Uhumbra on Dr. Lambert's recommended list, monitored me daily thanks to their on-site clinic. They both had ample experience caring for surrogate host species, although not human hosts specifically. Despite my being the first human surrogate for Uhumbra on record, their care set me at ease. Thus far, my health remained stable. Repeating that one-off incident in the Hôtel Mot-Valise became less and less of a concern. Also, Uhumbra fry had a reputation for being quite resilient, so there was little danger of their coming to harm inside the brood pouch unless I did something crazy. As for my balance, I just needed to be extra careful not to trip while walking and use the elevator whenever possible instead of stairs.

Accommodations at our hotel proved comfortable in every respect and included a swimming pool. As my pregnancy neared its conclusion, I found myself increasingly drawn to water. My doctors assured me this was normal for an Uhumbra surrogacy and to follow the instinct. Since Uhum frequently used host species for gestation, the hotel had plenty of surrogate swimwear to borrow. Surprisingly, the pool wasn't too busy, so I enjoyed bobbing around and floating in between swimming laps. That inner directive toward water became so strong that when the pool closed for the evening, I recreated the experience by swimming in our hotel room's ginormous bathtub. Dad didn't appreciate my hogging the bathroom, but I yelled through the door, "Pregnancy privileges!" He stomped off, muttering to himself or Mom.

Anyhow, the little ones seemed to approve of my extra swimming, and I found myself talking to them incessantly. A few times, I caught myself singing to them. They always became still during my renditions, making me wonder if they loved or hated them. Afterwards, they perked up again, swimming around inside me. They seemed especially active whenever I finished singing something by Neon Spark Plug. "Rock on, my little ones," I said, lying back in the tub with one hand resting on my middle. "You may not have my DNA, but you're definitely going to inherit my good taste in music. And you're only going to hear Durango Hacksaw's early work, back when they didn't suck."

As my time grew closer, I might as well have installed a seat belt on the toilet. Between almost hourly bowel movements and obsessive swimming, I had zero time to do anything else other than wolf down the occasional meal to keep the little ones from going berserk with hunger. By now, they had reached their full size, running out of room in the brood pouch. They still moved but definitely had less space to stretch their tiny bodies. Inside, I felt about ready to burst. But even though all those extra trips to the bathroom from incessant intestinal pressure annoyed me, there was something warm and fuzzy about the little ones' activity too. Their movements, no matter how subtle, made my skin tingle all over.

Meanwhile, Mom and Dad practiced for when they would need to take me to the nearby Tin'volk-uhum Sea for my delivery. The delivery site was about a mile from the hotel. When the time came, it would be easy to call my doctors and a cab. So, Mom's job was going to be monitoring my condition once I went into labor while Dad handled communications and transportation. Their division of tasks made sense. Dad had a commanding presence on the phone when ordering a cab, and Mom declared that her "feminine presence" would be more soothing when keeping me calm. Not that I expected to panic or anything, but I kind of agreed with Mom's reasoning. Considering that Dad got too upset to arrange prenatal care for me, he wouldn't be the best person for the job if I needed extra emotional support.

"I won't sugarcoat it, Henry," Mom said to me after she and Dad had another "labor drill," as they'd started calling it. "Giving birth is extremely painful. And it can be dangerous. That's why all three of us have Dr. Hollis and Dr. Nakurahan on speed dial. It's also why your father and I are practicing, so we can get you to the Tin'volk-uhum Sea safely and efficiently. I'm not saying any of this to scare you. I just want you to be prepared." She squeezed my hand and smiled. "And it's going to be okay."

"Yeah." I looked at my belly, expecting it to explode at any moment. The Uhumbra were packed in there so tightly, they barely moved all day. My most recent med-scan indicated they would be due any day now. "Dr. Nakurahan told me that the Uhumbra will use their pseudo-ovipositors to poke their way out of my belly button." *Something I'm definitely not looking forward to ...*

"That makes sense. I remember you telling me that the brood pouch is attached at the navel."

"Uh huh." I didn't really want to talk about it right now, not with my own mother, so I suggested we pray our family Rosary before going to one of the restaurants downstairs. Mom thought it was a great idea, and Dad joined us. Afterwards, while my parents dressed for dinner, I sat on the edge of my bed for a little private prayer session.

Jesus, Mary, and my Guardian Angel, it's almost my time, so I ask for your divine protection. Stroking the fullest part of my belly through the maternity shirt, I added, *I know that I'm forgiven now. So, I'm ready for whatever comes next. And I pray all the little ones come out okay and have good, long lives.*

Something squished inside, probably the little ones fighting each other for space. "Sorry," I said, petting them. My cheeks tingled, inducing a smile. "But you heard Dr. Hollis and Dr. Nakurahan. My brood pouch can't get any bigger, so you'll just have to make do with the limited space you have."

Tentacles scraped at the edges of my brood pouch. At least, that's what I thought they were. "Yeah, I know what it's like being cooped up. You know, before you guys came into existence, I was stuffed into a Zakonian jail cell with about twenty-four other men, and most of them were way bigger than me. We had to push our way around just to access the toilet, *one* toilet."

My mind drifted away from the little ones back to Zakon-4 State Jail. For a few minutes, the deplorable conditions of my captivity registered less forcefully in my brain than the fleeting connections forged there. Where was Traiyo now? And Polar Bear/Gorilla, and the Elbaren, and the two reptilian humanoid partners in crime? Most likely, I would never see any of them again. As that one famous cultural commentator so inanely said, "The universe is a big place." But wherever my former fellow prisoners were now, I prayed that they were safe and loved.

That night, while getting ready for bed after a light dinner and a long bathtub swim, something stabbed me in the gut. No, not stabbing – labor. I screamed from an equal combination of pain and surprise. Steadying myself against the nightstand, I called Dr. Hollis with my watch.

"It's happening." That was just about all I could say through my clenched teeth.

"Sit tight, Henry," Dr. Hollis said. "Dr. Nakurahan and I will be right up."

So much for Mom and Dad's methodical practice sessions. The minute they heard my outcry from the onset of labor, they literally stepped on each other's toes, barked orders, and generally scampered about like mice high on pharmaceuticals. It would have been comical if I didn't find myself lying on the floor beside the nightstand in agony with blood and water dripping from my navel. Seeing the blood threw me back to that cell at Kalka'ahn Maximum Security State Prison where the source of my current torment began. A flashback ensued of Alkamor's pseudo-ovipositor piercing my flesh to carry his young. It was my ticket out of death row, but the white-hot pain of labor made me wonder if I made the right choice.

Mom and Dad continued to argue in the hotel room, their worry turning to irritated shouts. *Do I have to be the clearheaded one right now?* I thought as I crawled out of the bedroom, scooting on my side to avoid putting direct pressure on the brood pouch. At least Mom had enough presence of mind to open the door for Dr. Hollis and Dr. Nakurahan when they knocked.

"You two, quit milling about," Dr. Nakurahan said to my parents, helping me to my feet. Only the doctor's strong tentacles managed to keep me from falling over as another labor pain shot through my middle, drawing a hellish scream from my core. "The cab is downstairs, ready to take you to Tin'volk-uhum."

"I don't know if I can make it." My legs shook from pain and sudden weakness. Another contraction like that would surely kill me. The two doctors supported me on either side while my parents followed close behind.

"You have to make it," Dr. Nakurahan said. "The fry must be delivered in Tin'volk-uhum." Just like Alkamor, my former cellmate and the biological parent of these children, Dr. Nakurahan had no bedside manner. Maybe that was an Uhumbra thing.

"Don't worry, Henry," Dr. Hollis said. "We'll get you there."

On the elevator ride to the lobby, I couldn't help screaming as another contraction hit. Shockingly, it was even worse than the last, rattling my entire body. Mom squeezed my hand, Dad rubbed my back, and the doctors kept me somewhat upright. Once in the lobby, I screamed some more. If anybody stared, I didn't notice. My only clear thought was to get into the cab and into the Tin'volk-uhum Sea a mile from the hotel. Saying a prayer didn't even occur to me.

In the cab, agony blinded me. I heard nothing, saw nothing, thought nothing. If my parents offered encouraging words or touches, I didn't notice. Nonstop moans, screams, and sobs escaped my throat. My tears could have filled a swimming pool. Pleas for divine mercy couldn't have passed through my lips if I tried. The little ones who once tumbled playfully inside the brood pouch turned murderous. Imagine two thousand needle-tipped knives concentrating on your navel, stabbing you over and over again, only stopping long enough to maximize the pain. That would feel far better than what I experienced during that cab ride to the sea. It was as though every inch of my abdominal flesh got cast into the nonstop tortures of hell.

Salt spray splashed my face. The full moon was too bright to look at straight on. I blinked, disoriented. *When did we get out of the cab?* Dr. Nakurahan tore off my bathrobe and pushed me into the ocean. Like I said, no bedside manner. Driven by some primal urge, I waded deeper and deeper – despite the agony – until I was nearly chest deep in water. Then, the pain stopped. *What the – ?*

Just like in those old Earth nature documentaries about seahorses giving birth, the Uhumbra pushed themselves out of my navel. Every contraction must have caused about a hundred to shoot out. In the moonlight, it was possible to see the little red creatures as they propelled out to sea. When all of the fry had come out, the brood pouch ejected and floated away with them, leaving my belly nearly flat again. Not one baby lingered. Out of the two thousand offspring, I figured at least one would swim back toward me, if only for a moment. The night before, I dreamed that some of the fry curled around my fingers to say goodbye, but that was just wishful thinking. I watched as the last of them dove beneath the water, disappearing for good. To them, I wasn't a parent, just a host. All those little tingly moments – the times they jumped about at mealtimes or quieted to listen to my songs – meant nothing.

As I waded to shore, all pain mysteriously gone, Dr. Nakurahan put my robe back on me. I stumbled out of the water toward Dr. Hollis and my parents. All of them spoke, but I didn't hear anything. My mind fixated on the roaring tide that pulled the little ones farther and farther away, where I would never see them again. At some point, my family must have guided me into the cab and taken me back to the hotel, but that memory remains inaccessible. And they must have comforted me in our hotel room, but I have no recollection of that either. All I remember was that after giving birth in the Tin'volk-uhum Sea, I lay in my hotel room bed staring at the ceiling for more than two hours, bawling my eyes out.

Acknowledgements

Thank you to the team at WPP for giving Henry Trevalu's harrowing mpreg misadventure a good home.

About the Author

E.J. LeRoy is a Pushcart Prize nominated writer and poet whose work has appeared in several publications including *Adventures Bookzine*, *Horrific Scribes*, *Neon Dystopia*, *NonBinary Review*, and *Permanent Flux*. Henry Trevalu is a recurring character whose intergalactic misadventures are cataloged here: https://ejleroy.weebly.com/series.html

www.ingramcontent.com/pod-product-compliance
Lightning Source LLC
LaVergne TN
LVHW051007080826
845145LV00009B/2498

* 9 7 8 1 9 5 9 3 3 0 4 2 4 *